SOCCER DUEL

WITHDRAWN

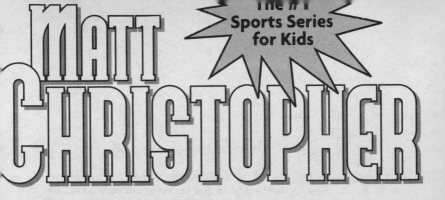

MATT CHRISTOPHER

The #1 Sports Series for Kids

SOCCER DUEL

Text by Paul Mantell

LB 1837

Little, Brown and Company
Boston   New York   London

First Edition

Library of Congress Cataloging-in-Publication Data

Mantell, Paul.
    Soccer Duel / Paul Mantell.
        p.   cm.
    Summary: Team rivalry threatens to spoil a budding friendship between a showy soccer player, Bryce, and soft-spoken but talented Renny.
    ISBN 0-316-13474-0 (hc) — ISBN 0-316-13406-6 (pb)
    [1. Soccer — Fiction.]   I. Title.
PZ7.C458Snt   2000
[Fic] — dc21   99-048070

10 9 8 7 6 5

COM-MO

Printed in the United States of America

To Barbara, Mark, Tim, and Renee

SOCCER DUEL

Renny Harding was running as fast as he could. He was panting, his heart pounding in his ears, as he whizzed by the houses and trees on the way to Woodman Field. He was late for his Saturday morning soccer game!

He had never been late before. There must have been a blackout overnight, because his alarm clock had been blinking 12:00 when he woke up. He'd flown out of bed when he'd checked his wristwatch and seen that it was quarter to eight.

He had an eight o'clock game!

His mom was sleeping. Normally, she would have been on her way to work at the real estate agency (Saturdays were big days showing houses to prospective buyers). But she'd come down with some kind of virus and had called last night to say she wouldn't be in today.

Renny had thought about waking her up and asking her to drive him, but he knew she needed to stay in bed and rest. Besides, Woodman Field was only five blocks away, and by the time she got up and dressed, he figured, he could have been there and back. So he just put on his uniform and ran out the door, full speed.

He pulled up for a breather just a block short of the field. From here, he could see that the game hadn't started yet. Renny blew out a relieved breath. The teams were still warming up. He hadn't missed the opening whistle.

"I don't know why you bother running. You're only going to ride the bench anyway," came a familiar voice.

Renny looked up and saw his friend Norm Harvey sitting on the porch of his house, playing chess with his dad.

"You never know," Renny said, still huffing and puffing, his hands on his hips. "Today might be my big chance."

"Give me a break," Norm said, rolling his eyes.

"When do you ever get to play more than ten minutes a game? That's not much time to make an impression on your coach."

Renny scowled. "I'm a little late," he muttered and turned to go.

Norm Harvey had been his first friend in Crestmont when Renny and his mom had moved from Haverford in October. Norm had befriended him at a low point in his life. In fact, he'd been Renny's only friend for months.

But now it was spring, and thanks to soccer, Renny had started to make other friends — ones he had more in common with. He and Norm had drifted apart lately.

It suddenly occurred to Renny that maybe Norm was feeling bad about that. Renny hadn't called him to go to a movie or bowling in weeks — not since soccer season started.

Renny stopped and turned. "Hey, Norm, want to go play miniature golf this afternoon?" he suggested.

Norm immediately brightened up. "Can I, Dad?" he asked his father.

"Sure," said Norm's dad. "Do you guys need me to take you?"

Renny nodded gratefully. He missed his own dad a lot. He hadn't seen him more than a few times since the divorce. Sometimes he felt like his dad didn't care about him anymore — even though he knew it wasn't true. His dad was just very busy, and every time he did come around, he had a fight with Renny's mom. It was no fun for any of them.

Renny liked Norm's family. They always did stuff together.

"You want to come watch my game?" he suddenly blurted out.

Norm looked away. "Well, maybe a little later," he said. "After we finish our game here." He indicated the chessboard.

Renny knew Norm was being nice, trying to spare his feelings. Norm hated all sports. Miniature golf was about as athletic as he got, so Renny never suggested having a catch together or kicking a ball around.

But what Norm had to understand was how much Renny loved sports. Back in Haverford, he'd been one of the best players in his soccer league. When he and his mom had come to Crestmont after the divorce settlement he'd hoped he'd be able to play fall soccer. But they'd moved right in the middle of the season, and it was too late for Renny to sign up. So he'd spent the fall watching from the sidelines rather than running on the field.

No one in Crestmont knew that Renny could play the game. And no one *would* know as long as Coach McMaster kept him on the bench. With a deep sigh, Renny resumed his trot toward the soccer field.

"There you are, Renny!" Coach McMaster said, looking up from his lineup chart. "Okay, we'll get you in before halftime." Renny nodded and sat down on the bench, just as the opening whistle sounded and the game began.

Back in Haverford, Renny had been an all-star center striker, the position right in the middle of the front line usually given to the team's best shooter. Renny wasn't the biggest kid on his team — far from it. In a league where some kids had already hit their growth spurt, he was barely average in height. He was skinny, too, although well built. He was fast and agile, and although he didn't have the strongest shot, he was accurate and had great "deke" moves. As he'd tried to tell Coach McMaster when the team had shown up for its first spring practice, he had been the second-highest goal scorer in his old league.

But the Blue Hornets' coach hadn't really paid attention. He had his team from the fall league back again, and he wasn't going to sit any of them down in favor of some new kid. So Renny had started the season on the bench, waiting for his chance.

Now, three-quarters through the season, he was still sitting out most games. When he did get in, he never got to play center striker. Never. Coach McMaster put him in on defense. Defense! Back in Haverford, he'd never played defense, even once! No wonder the coach didn't think he could play the game.

"Norm is right," Renny murmured under his breath, discouraged. "Why do I even bother?" The moment the words left his mouth, he wanted to take them back. Renny prided himself on being a team player, no matter what. So he squared his shoulders and turned his attention to the game.

Out on the field, the other team, the Yellow Jackets, had just scored a goal.

"That was fast," Jordan Woo said. Jordan rode the

bench every game along with Renny. Renny couldn't figure out why Jordan kept coming back for more. Unlike Renny, he was not an athlete. Renny liked Jordan — they had a lot of classes together at school and got along fine — but he hated being grouped with Jordan in people's minds as someone who couldn't play soccer.

"Who scored?" Renny asked. "I wasn't watching."

"Bryce McCormack, who else?" Jordan commented, making a face. "We might as well give up now and avoid the embarrassment. We're not gonna beat the Yellow Jackets. They're undefeated, you know."

"So what?" Renny shot back. "The game's not over — they haven't beaten us yet."

Renny watched the standings as much as any of his teammates on the Blue Hornets. After all, what else was there to talk about on the bench except the game, people's stats, the upcoming schedule, and the standings? "Anyway, we don't have to play them again after this, do we?" he asked Jordan.

"Only if we make the play-offs," Jordan said, with a look that said "fat chance."

"I don't know — if we beat them today, we could make it," Renny pointed out. "Isaac Mendez is right up there with Bryce McCormack."

"No way!" Jordan protested. "Bryce is in a league of his own. Besides, we'd have to beat the Red Scorpions and the Orange Crush to get to the championships. No way that's going to happen."

"I still say we can do it," Renny insisted. Why did Jordan have to be so negative? he wondered. It was the worst thing about him. Other than that, he was a pretty nice kid. But Renny couldn't stand that attitude. It was a loser attitude as far as he was concerned. You were beaten before you started. He opened his mouth to say so.

At that instant, a roar went up from the other side of the field as Bryce McCormack scored again. "Yeah? You still say what?" Jordan asked, arching one eyebrow.

Renny looked away, focusing on the game instead of Jordan and his sarcastic remarks.

Play had resumed. The Blue Hornets were on the defensive now, scrambling to regroup. Two or three of them wanted to hover around Bryce McCormack all the time, even though it meant they were way out of position and that other Yellow Jackets were unguarded. But Bryce McCormack didn't seem to notice the defenders or need his teammates at all. Like a one-man team, he kept possession of the ball, dribbling masterfully, weaving in and out among the defenders while advancing toward the Blue Hornets' goal.

Renny looked on in admiration. Bryce was an amazing player. Renny wondered if he could ever be that good.

Bryce got off a good shot, but it bounced off the post and into the goalie's arms. The goalie, Chuck Mathes, kicked it back out to midfield, where the Hornets' midfielder, Travis Blumenthal, was waiting for it. He quickly kicked it forward to Isaac Mendez, the Hornets' center striker, who raced upfield. With only one defenseman and the goalie to beat, it looked as if he might have a chance to even the score.

Isaac tried to deke as the sole defender leaped forward. But one of the defender's feet snagged Isaac, tripping him up. Isaac landed hard, his ankle twisted in an unnatural position. Isaac yelled in pain, the whistle blew, and a half dozen adults rushed onto the field.

Anyone watching could see that this was a serious injury. Renny stood up but made no move. He was horrified by what he'd just seen. The ankle had to be broken; there was no doubt about it. He sat back down slowly and rested his head in his hands. He was suddenly queasy, imagining how Isaac Mendez must have felt at the instant he hit the turf.

Slowly, Isaac was taken off the field and lifted into a waiting car. As Renny watched the car pull out of the parking lot, he felt a hand on his shoulder and looked up to see Coach McMaster staring down at him.

"You ready to go in?" he asked Renny.

"Me?" Renny replied, surprised. "What about John Singleman?" he asked, referring to the team's second stringer.

"Gone for the weekend with his family," the coach said. "Didn't you notice he wasn't here?"

Renny shook his head dumbly. He hadn't noticed. And now *he* was going into the game — as center striker! Renny felt a wave of happiness come over him, followed immediately by a sharp pang of guilt. Isaac Mendez was hurt, maybe badly. Renny had no right to be happy about it. Still, he knew this was his big chance — the moment he'd been waiting for all season.

"I asked if you were ready," the coach reminded him.

Renny took a deep breath and nodded. "I'm ready," he said, looking Coach McMaster in the eye.

The coach gave him a little shove, sending him out onto the field. "Come on, Hornets!" he shouted. "Do it for Isaac!"

The Blue Hornets let out a cheer and took their positions. The ref blew his whistle, and the game was on again.

2

Who's that kid?" Bryce McCormack wanted to know. He paced the sidelines like a caged lion.

"I don't know," Eric Dornquist said. "One of their subs, I think."

"Well, he's running rings around our defense," Bryce complained. "Come on, defense!" he yelled, as his teammates tried in vain to stay with the Hornet sub. "Look out, he's gonna score . . . !" Bryce's voice trailed off as the newcomer slipped the ball past the outmaneuvered Yellow Jackets goalie.

"Who *is* that kid?" Bryce asked again.

"Number Seven," Eric replied.

"I can see that," Bryce said with a scowl. "Go over to their bench at halftime and find out, okay?"

"Sure," Eric said. "Anything you say, Bryce."

Bryce knew his teammates were afraid of his temper — and that was fine with him. His occasional flare-ups had helped get them this far, hadn't they? Undefeated, with a record of 6–0. First place, and a lock to make the play-offs if they won just one of their remaining games. That wouldn't be any trouble, since most of their opponents were the league's bottom-feeders, teams that should be pushovers for the Yellow Jackets.

With Isaac Mendez out, the Blue Hornets should have been a pushover, too. But who was this new kid they had playing for them? He had to be the fastest player in the whole league. And that was a great move he'd put on the defenders, Bryce had to admit.

"Put me back in, Coach," Bryce demanded.

"Too late, Bryce," Coach Hickey replied with a shake of his head. "Halftime's coming up — hey, look out; defense!" He suddenly turned his attention back to the field, where once again, the new kid was cutting through the bewildered Yellow Jackets defensive line.

"Come on!" Bryce yelled at the top of his lungs. "Wake up out there!" He winced as the new kid made as if to shoot. The Yellow Jackets' goalie, Sam

Plummer, leaped into the air to block the shot —
but the kid had faked him out. The ball was still rest-
ing at his feet. All he had to do was give the ball a
gentle nudge. It rolled slowly into the net, just a second ahead of Sam's sliding dive.

The ref blew his whistle twice to signal the end of
the first half. "Tie game!" Bryce moaned. "I told you
to put me back in there, Coach!"

"Look, Bryce," Coach Hickey said with annoy-
ance, "you're not on defense anyway. I'll get you in
there next half, okay? Meanwhile, adjust your attitude."

Bryce skulked off and poured himself a cup of wa-
ter from the cooler. He stood drinking it as Eric
Dornquist ran toward him from across the field.

"It's Renny Harding," he said, out of breath.

"What?" Bryce turned a disbelieving eye on Eric.
"That little runt is in my science class. The kid's a
nerd!"

"Yeah, well, he can play soccer, wouldn't you say?"
Eric pointed out.

"Hmmm . . ." Bryce grunted, then tossed his paper cup onto the field, ignoring the nearby trash can.

Ten minutes later, the ref blew his whistle to signal the start of the second half. "Come on, let's go on out there and swat some Blue Hornets," Bryce yelled as he ran onto the field, as psyched as he had ever been in his life.

But the second half of the game left him feeling totally frustrated. Bryce kept standing there, free and unguarded in the Hornets' zone, while the ball remained in the Yellow Jackets' own end, fought over by players from both teams. Every time the ball seemed about to come out to him, it was intercepted — most of the time by that kid Renny.

When Renny took control of the ball in the last minute of play, with the score still tied, Bryce finally gave up. He ran for his own end, determined not to let the runt score again.

Renny was dribbling his way around three defenders, all of whom looked as if they were rooted to the ground. Bryce came up behind him and cut off his escape route. Renny was now surrounded by Yellow Jackets, right in front of their goal.

The final whistle was going to blow any second, Bryce thought with satisfaction. No way the kid gets a shot off. It's only a tie, but hey, we can live with that.

But Renny had one final trick up his sleeve. He lifted the ball along his leg with his foot, then hopped up into the air, sending the ball skyward. At the top of its arc, he headed it over the defenders to a surprised Hornets forward. The forward managed to get his foot on it, and before anyone knew what was happening, the winning shot was past the goalie, the whistle had blown ending the game, and Renny's blue-shirted teammates were mobbing him, whooping and hollering.

Bryce cursed to himself, blinking back tears of rage and humiliation. Finding the ball rolling slowly toward him, he wound up his leg and kicked it so far into the woods surrounding the field that no one would ever find it.

It was his team's first defeat — and it had come at the hands of some scrub nobody'd even paid attention to before! Bryce gritted his teeth and stared at Renny, who was being lifted onto his cheering teammates' shoulders.

"You got lucky this game, kid," he murmured under his breath. "But I'm going to figure you out. Nobody beats Bryce McCormack on a soccer field. Nobody."

3

Soccer is exactly like chess — well, sort of," Renny tried to explain to Norm as the two boys walked down Jermyn Street on their way to Conroy's Luncheonette. It was a bright, sunny afternoon. It had been hot playing miniature golf, making them thirsty for Conroy's ice-cream sodas, the best in the whole county.

"What do you mean, it's like chess?" Norm retorted. "I'm outraged! That is a total insult to the thousands of grand masters over thousands of years whose collective wisdom goes into every move Kasparov makes!"

"Who?"

"The chess champion of the world, duh!" Norm said. "Everybody in the world knows Kasparov."

"No, Norm. Everybody in the world does not

know Kasparov. Everybody in the world knows Maradona. Mia Hamm. Manchester United. The World Cup. Soccer, the world's number one sport. That, everybody knows."

"So say you. When history looks back, it will conclude that sports of the brain were definitely cooler than sports of the body," Norm said with a fake British accent, and both boys cracked up.

That was the thing Renny liked best about Norm — his sense of humor. Being a brain and not an athlete meant Norm was a target for bullies. Renny knew Norm's wit was a useful weapon against them — by the time other kids got through laughing, they mostly didn't feel like teasing Norm anymore.

"Ah, we're here!" Norm said as they walked into the air-conditioned coolness of Conroy's. Renny led the way to the bar, and they plunked down on a pair of red rotating stools.

"What'll it be?" asked Conroy, a big bald man with a fringe of white hair and a walrus mustache. Renny didn't know if Conroy was his first or last name; everyone just called him Conroy. Conroy's place was more than just a luncheonette — it was a piece of the past. It sold old-fashioned candy by the pound and served homemade ice cream. On the back wall was a huge painting of a farm that made it seem as if you were looking out the front windows of a farmhouse, watching cows munching on grass and chickens pecking the ground.

"Two ice-cream sodas — choco-van," Renny said.

"The usual, huh?" Conroy said with a laugh. He got busy making their sodas.

"So go on," Norm said. "You were saying how soccer is just like chess?"

"Okay, what I mean is, they're both popular all over the world and they both use strategy."

"You could say that about a lot of things," Norm pointed out. "But I could never be good at soccer."

"Who said you have to be good at something to appreciate it?" Renny argued. "For instance, that second goal I scored today —"

"Oh boy, here we go again," Norm interrupted. "You score a couple of goals, and now I have to hear about it forever. No, go ahead, I insist. It's all so fascinating."

Renny frowned. Norm didn't realize what a big

day this had been for him. "All season, I've been sitting on the bench, Norm. You ought to know what that feels like."

"Oh, I do," Norm said. "That's why I don't play soccer."

Useless, Renny realized. Norm was never going to get it about soccer. Too bad. If he really understood the game, he'd see that you had to think ahead, to anticipate your opponent's next move and outmaneuver the other guy — just like in chess.

Conroy put their ice-cream sodas in front of them. "Enjoy," he said with a smile, and went over to deal with another group of customers. Looking up, Renny saw that one of them was Bryce McCormack.

"Ugh. I hate that kid Bryce," Norm said softly. "He once bounced a soccer ball off the back of my head in third grade."

For a second, Renny felt the urge to laugh, picturing the ball ricocheting off Norm's head. But he stifled himself, realizing with a pang how much it must have hurt Norm's feelings. "That was a long time ago," he said instead. "Maybe he's changed."

"Yeah? Well, I'll tell you one thing — it's never

going to happen again, because I'm never getting on another soccer field, and I don't think I'll be getting into advanced P.E. any time soon."

Renny looked over Norm's shoulder at Bryce, who glanced up and saw him. "Hey!" Bryce called out with a smile and a wave. "How you doin'?"

"Fine, thanks," Renny said, surprised.

Bryce gave Conroy his order, then got up and came slowly over to Renny and Norm. "Nice game today," he told Renny, offering his hand.

Renny was taken off guard. He would have thought he was the last person Bryce would want to talk to, seeing as how he'd just helped ruin the Yellow Jackets' undefeated record. But it seemed just the opposite; Bryce appeared eager to talk to him.

So Renny shook Bryce's hand. "Thanks," he replied.

"'Scuse me," Norm mumbled, slipping off his stool. "I've gotta go to the bathroom." From behind Bryce's back, Norm made like he was throwing up.

Bryce didn't notice. "Excellent game," he told Renny, nodding his head seriously.

"Thanks," Renny said, flattered. He'd been congratulated a lot in the past few hours, and getting

21

hoisted on his teammates' shoulders was something he would never forget. But hearing it from Bryce, arguably the league's best player, meant a lot.

Renny noticed Bryce squinting at him in a weird way, as if he was sizing him up. Suddenly, Renny felt uncomfortable, and a little scared. "You played good, too," he offered.

"Not good enough," Bryce said flatly. "You played better than me."

Now what am I supposed to say to that? Renny wondered. "I don't know about that. . . ." he said, feeling his face redden.

"Your team won, didn't it?" Bryce insisted. "That means you played better, bottom line — that's it; no buts." He squinted at Renny again. "So, how come I never heard you could play?"

"Well, I've only lived here for eight months," Renny explained. "I played center striker where I used to live, but, you know . . . here, I ride the bench because the Hornets have Isaac Mendez."

"*Had* Isaac Mendez," Bryce corrected, shaking his head. "His ankle's broken. You can forget about him this season."

Renny hadn't heard the news, and suddenly he was in a confusion of emotion. He felt terrible for Isaac but elated at the same time. He was now second-string center striker, right behind John Singleman. From now on, for at least a few minutes every game, he would actually get to play his favorite position!

Guilt washed over Renny. Only a real lowlife would be happy to hear that Isaac's ankle had been broken.

Bryce must have read Renny's expression wrong, because he said, "Don't worry about losing Isaac. The way you played, your team still has a shot at the play-offs. You beat *us,* right?"

There was something strange in the tone of Bryce's voice. Something angry, something unsatisfied. But it quickly passed. "Anyway, like I said, you're really good, Harding. It was painful watching you beat us."

Bryce smiled then — a real smile. "They should have put me in on defense. I would have stopped you." He clapped Renny on the shoulder. "See you in the play-offs, huh?"

"Hope so," Renny said. They gave each other five, and Bryce went back to his stool at the far end of the bar.

Renny sipped his ice-cream soda and stared straight ahead, imagining the future.... *He was the star center striker of the Blue Hornets . . . they were in the play-offs, fighting it out against Bryce McCormack's Yellow Jackets. The two stars were best friends off the field, archrivals on it. . . .*

Norm returned from the bathroom. "What did jerko want?" he asked, bending over his straw and sipping his soda.

"Just to tell me 'good game,'" Renny said.

"He's up to something," Norm warned Renny. "Trust me; I've known him longer than you."

"Come on, Norm. Lighten up, will you? Lose the black cloud." He gave Norm a gentle push on the arm, sending him spinning around on his stool.

But for an instant, as he thought about what Norm had said, Renny wondered if his chess-playing friend might be right. Something about that tone in Bryce's voice . . .

4

"Well? What do you think?" Eric Dornquist asked as Bryce sat back down on his stool. "Is the kid for real or not?"

Bryce gave his teammate a long look and a slow smile. Then he waved to Renny Harding and his nerd friend Norm, who were leaving Conroy's. Bryce smiled wider, remembering how funny Norm had looked that time in third grade when he'd hit him in the head with a soccer ball.

Bryce swiveled back around to look at Eric. "Harding's a one-shot wonder," he said. "He took us by surprise, that's all. Once people realize he's fast and start paying attention to him, he won't be able to get off a good shot. Even if he does, he doesn't get much on the kick. I mean, just look at him. He's not exactly gigantic."

Eric laughed. Bryce relaxed and enjoyed the moment. He remembered how thrilled Renny had been that Bryce had even talked to him. Ha! That smile when he'd told the kid how great he was? The kid would be a pushover if they ever met on the field again.

"No, I'm pretty sure today's game was a fluke. Come on — the kid wasn't even second-string on his team!" Bryce laughed. "Anyway, we'd better get the word out, so the other teams know about him."

"Who are they playing next?" Eric asked.

Bryce took out the schedule he always kept in his back pocket. It had taken a beating over the long weeks of the season, but it was still semi-readable.

"Only two more regular-season games," Bryce said. "They play the Red Scorpions and the Orange Crush." The sly smile broke out on his face again. "No way they make the play-offs. They have to beat both those teams, and there is no possible way, now that Isaac Mendez is out for the season."

"You're sure Renny Harding doesn't pose a threat?" Eric asked.

Bryce smiled. "As sure as I'm sittin' here. I'm gonna stick around after our game next week, just to

26

watch him get stung by the Scorpions. Yeah. I'm gonna enjoy seeing that."

Bryce threw some money down on the bar to cover his ice-cream soda, then left Conroy's. It was time to head back home. He had some phone calls to make.

"Hey, McCormack!" A strong hand grabbed Bryce by the shoulder and spun him around.

"Jake Henry!" Bryce shook hands with Crestmont High School's all-star goalie. Jake was only a sophomore, but he was already starting for the varsity squad and was on his way to being all-county.

"Listen — who are you playin' next week?"

"The Black Jacks," Bryce told him. "We'll mop the floor with them. Why?"

"You'd better play good, dude. 'Cause Coach Harrelson is gonna be there."

"Coach Harrelson?" Bryce straightened up, paying close attention now. "He's coming to see the Town League games?"

"He's scouting for this fall's junior varsity squad. And I told him to watch out for you; said you were center striker material."

Bryce felt his heart hammering. He grinned from

ear to ear, proud as he could be. "Thanks!" he said to Jake.

"De nada," Jake said. "Don't mention it. You've got the goods. I didn't lie to the man."

"Cool," was all Bryce could say. He could see himself now, a freshman starting for the junior varsity team at center striker!

"Like I told you," Jake added as he opened the door to Conroy's. "It's your big chance to impress him — so don't depress him, all right?"

"I hear you," Bryce said. "Thanks for the heads up."

"Just be good. I talked the talk. Now you gotta walk the walk."

Jake disappeared inside. Bryce took a deep breath, blowing it out slowly. Coach Harrelson was coming to see him play! And Jake had already built him up way high — maybe too high, Bryce realized. It would have been better to surprise the coach, coming out of nowhere, with no expectations — the way that kid Renny had done it today.

Now Coach Harrelson would already be expecting Bryce to play like a star. Bryce felt a coil of fear creep up his spine. He couldn't win! If he played great, the coach would have already been expecting it. And if he didn't play well? If he didn't score a single goal against the lowly Black Jacks?

Bryce didn't even want to think about it. He trudged off toward home, the ice-cream soda he'd just finished churning in his stomach.

So in order to qualify for the championship round, your team simply has to win its last two games, is that it?"

"You have the makings of a great team statistician!" Renny said, clapping Norm on the back. "We really need to know stuff like that, but we don't have time to figure it out."

"Thanks, but no thanks," Norm said. "Be grateful I'm coming along with you today." The two boys walked side by side toward the field. It was the following Saturday, and Renny had finally talked Norm into watching him play.

"Hey, isn't that Bryce McJerk on the field?" Norm asked, suddenly hanging back. "You told me he wasn't going to be here."

"I said we're not playing his team," Renny corrected him. "His game must just be ending."

But it wasn't. It was only the start of the second half, as they soon found out. Play had been delayed because the ref's car wouldn't start that morning.

"What's the score?" Renny asked John Singleman, who was standing on the sidelines.

"Six–three Yellow Jackets," John told him. "Bryce has four goals. Oops. Make that five."

A roar had gone up from one side of the field, where the Yellow Jackets and their fans were whooping it up. Bryce pumped his fists into the air and ran down the field, then went into a triumphant slide, shimmying to a stop.

"That kid is a one-man team," said a man standing next to Renny. The man wrote some notes on a pad he was carrying. He frowned and shook his head. Renny thought the man looked familiar.

"Hey." He nudged Norm. "Who's that guy?"

"That guy?" Norm looked past Renny. "That's Coach Harrelson."

"The high school coach?" Renny breathed, turning

to sneak another peek before the coach looked up from his pad.

"He's checking out players for next year's junior varsity squad, I heard," John Singleman said. "You play like you did last week and he's gonna notice."

Renny gave an embarrassed laugh. "I probably won't even play much. You're first-string now; I'm just subbing for you."

"Nuh-uh," John said, shaking his head. "Didn't you hear? Coach is going with you first half. He's gonna ride the hot hand."

"Huh?" Renny couldn't believe his ears.

"You're starting, man!" John told him. "I'm moving over to left wing to make room for you. Hey, I hear you were awesome last week!"

Renny still couldn't believe he was starting. If only his mom or his dad were here!

He looked again at Coach Harrelson. "He said Bryce McCormack was a one-man team," he said to John Singleman.

"Well, he is," John acknowledged. "That kid is good. Trouble is, he knows it. Get what I mean?"

"*I* get what you mean," Norm broke in.

Renny was too preoccupied to react to Norm's comment. He was starting at center striker today! He looked out onto the field, watching Bryce move with the ball, bowling over defenders with his combination of aggressiveness and size.

"I could never be as good as him," Renny murmured under his breath. "Plus he's got that killer shot." As if to punctuate Renny's thought, Bryce put a monster shot past the goalie's left shoulder for his sixth goal of the game.

Renny knew that his own strengths were his speed, his moves, and his ability to think ahead and be in the right place. Those were all good things, but could they substitute for size, aggressiveness, and a killer shot?

Renny looked at Coach Harrelson, who was writing in his book again, shaking his head and frowning.

"He can't believe how good Bryce is," Renny whispered, awestruck. "Who could believe it? And Bryce is having the game of his life besides."

Renny sighed, wishing he were bigger, meaner, more of a banger, more like Bryce. It would have been nice to be the one Coach Harrelson wrote about in his little scouting book.

6

Bryce stood on the sidelines at the end of the game. He should have been celebrating, but instead he was feeling confused and a little hurt. He'd scored six goals — six goals! And Coach Harrelson had barely even congratulated him. "Nice job, son," he'd told Bryce. "You're gonna be a good one."

What did he mean, "gonna be"? Bryce wondered. What was he right now — chopped liver? Six goals!

The second game had started with barely a minute's break, because the whole day had been thrown behind schedule. Bryce noticed that Coach Harrelson had stayed to watch it.

Bryce saw a soccer ball lying there and felt the urge to smash it a hundred yards down the field, but he restrained himself. Coach Harrelson had probably just gone easy on the compliments. He probably hadn't wanted Bryce to get a swelled head. Okay, he could handle that.

Bryce glanced at Coach Harrelson. The JV coach was staring at someone on the field. Bryce followed his gaze downfield, where Renny was dribbling the ball into the Red Scorpions' zone.

Renny was covered by three men. Bryce smiled humorlessly. The Scorpions must have heard about Renny's last game. "Try and score now, shrimp," Bryce muttered softly.

At the last minute, though, Renny deked right, drawing the defenders off balance, then passed a perfect thread-the-needle to his open left-winger, John Singleman. Singleman shot home the goal.

Bryce grimaced.

"Now that's unselfish play. Hey, McMaster, who is that kid at center striker?"

Bryce's gaze snapped back to Coach Harrelson.

"Renny Harding," the Blue Hornets' coach replied. "New in town this year. He's subbing for Isaac Mendez."

"The kid with the ankle? Too bad about that. I wanted to get a look at him. But this kid's pretty good! I like the way he found the open man."

Bryce could practically feel the steam coming out of his ears. That stupid kid Renny again! Stealing all the attention away from where it rightfully belonged. How many goals had Renny scored this season, anyway? Nowhere near his own total, that was for sure.

As if he'd read Bryce's mind, Renny scored his first goal of the game moments later. It came off a give-and-go play, in which Renny passed off to John Singleman, then immediately rushed forward. The winger quickly kicked the ball back into Renny's path, and Renny faked the goalie out before guiding the ball home.

"What a lucky shot!" Bryce growled, his voice drowned out by the roar from the Hornets' sideline. "He barely got anything on it!"

"Yes," said a voice next to him. "But it still counts. Sometimes brute force isn't the best way to get what you want."

Bryce turned to see who had spoken, and saw Norm Harvey staring up at him with a huge grin. Bryce wanted to say something nasty to him, but Coach Harrelson was standing right there. Shut up, Bryce mouthed silently.

"What? Can't hear you," Norm said innocently.

". . . and he's not a hot dog like that other kid in the first game," Bryce heard Coach Harrelson say.

The words hit Bryce like a punch in the gut. Stung in every fiber of his being, he stormed off, promising himself that he would get even with Renny Harding, and his geeky friend Norm, too — if it was the last thing he ever did.

Bryce stared at page 256 of his math textbook. He stared and stared. He hadn't done a problem for several minutes. He just sat there, thinking about that same horrible moment over and over again. Hearing Coach Harrelson's voice as he said, "Not a hot dog like that other kid," meaning him, Bryce. His high school soccer career had ended right there. All his dreams right up in smoke. All because of that stupid Renny Harding!

Since he was three years old, Bryce had impressed everyone with his athletic skills. He was good at everything he tried, but at soccer he was in a class by himself. It had always been that way — till now.

It hadn't occurred to Bryce that someday he

might not be the best anymore, that all the attention he'd always gotten might end up going to someone else. Now it was Renny Harding who would be the new high school soccer sensation. Bryce would be nothing. A substitute. A lowly second-string scrub.

His eyes came back into focus at the sound of his mother's voice. "Bryce?" she called from upstairs. "It's nine-thirty. How 'bout getting up to bed, huh?"

"Soon," Bryce heard himself say. He forced himself to concentrate on his homework until he'd finished it. Then he went up to bed and lay there in the dark, picturing that same moment, over and over and over again.

There had to be a way out of this nightmare. A way to make sure he would still be the best . . .

At lunch period the next day, Bryce sat down next to Turk Walters. "Hey, Turk," he said. "I've been looking all over for you."

"I'm not too hard to find," Turk said.

It was the truth, all right. He was at least six foot two, with the build of a wrestler and bright red hair. He played defense for the Orange Crush. Turk wasn't exactly Sir Speedy, but he was big and aggressive, and a scary force on the soccer field — which was exactly why Bryce had sought him out.

"I wanted to talk to you about something."

"I'm listening." Turk stuffed half a tuna salad sandwich into his mouth. He started chewing, and the bulge in his cheeks was so big it was hard for Bryce to concentrate.

"Mmphghmfgm?" Turk said, motioning for Bryce to go ahead.

"Um, you know how you guys are playing the Blue Hornets this Sunday?"

"Mphgm." Turk nodded yes.

"You know that kid Renny Harding who's filling in for Isaac Mendez at center striker?"

"Phmphmgh?" Turk said, giving a "What about him?" motion.

"I just wanted to clue you in about him — because I know if you guys beat them, you go to the play-offs instead of them. And you know I want you and me to meet for the trophy, man."

Turk's eyes bugged excitedly, and he gave a vigorous nod. "Mphgph!" he said.

"Okay, so this kid Renny, I don't know if you've ever seen him. He's a little runty kid, about this high, and kind of skinny. You could whip him in two seconds."

Turk laughed, losing a crumb or two of his sandwich, and nodded again. He finally swallowed his food and wiped his mouth on his sleeve. "Or I could just sit on him," he said, chuckling again and sending a spit shower into the air.

Bryce wiped off his face with a napkin and tried to forget what he was wiping. "The thing is, he's a wimp, you know?" he told Turk. "If you foul him hard a couple of times right at the start, he'll get all shook up. You scare him, he's meat. Got it?"

"Oh, I got it, all right," Turk said, slapping Bryce five. "I'm gonna send him to intensive care! That kid is toast. Come down on Sunday and watch me whip him."

Bryce smiled, getting up. "I wouldn't miss it for anything," he said. "See you there — and see you in the play-offs."

He left Turk sitting with the rest of his lunch. Good. He'd done what he could. He'd planted the seed. Now it was up to Turk Walters to do an Orange Crush on Renny Harding.

7

Two days after the victory over the Scorpions, Renny still smiled whenever he thought about the game. Only one thing interfered with his good mood — his parents.

When he'd returned home on Saturday after the game, he'd called his mom at work to tell her the good news. He knew she was proud of him, but she'd been on her car phone so she hadn't been able to talk much.

Longing to tell someone else about the game, Renny called his father. When he got the answering machine, he sighed and left a message asking his father to call him back as soon as he could.

His father did call back, but not until dinnertime. His mother answered the phone. She was tired from working, and the tone in her voice was snappish —

the very tone his father had complained endlessly about in the months before the divorce.

"He's eating dinner right now," his mother said. Renny looked up from his empty plate. "Why are you calling?"

Her brow furrowed as she listened. "Oh, he called you, did he?" She cast a sidelong glance at Renny. "Well, of course he'd have to call you, since you never call him first."

There was a long pause during which her mouth got tighter and tighter. Finally, she said curtly, "You tell him yourself." She handed the phone to Renny.

"Uh, hi, Dad. Thanks for calling back," Renny said. "I wanted to tell you about my game today." His mother picked up his plate and busied herself at the sink. Renny could tell she was steaming mad about something, but he was too eager to tell his dad about the game to take much notice.

He recapped it as best he could. He tried not to make his role come off as too important, but he *had* been the only one to score, so he had to mention that, didn't he?

His father congratulated him enthusiastically,

then paused. Renny remembered that there was something his father wanted to tell him. Something bad, he guessed — correctly, as it turned out.

"Listen, Renny," his father said, his voice full of apology. "I know I promised to join you on the trail cleanup project this Saturday, but I can't be there after all. I have to go out of town on business. But I'll make it up to you soon, okay?"

"Out of town on business." Renny's mom had hated the amount of time his dad was away. Now Renny could see her point. But he knew it was useless to say anything, so he just mumbled that he understood.

"I'll see you soon, though, right, Dad?" he added, trying not to see how his mother's back stiffened.

"You bet," his dad replied. "As soon as I can. See you, Renny." And with that, his father hung up.

Renny returned the phone to its cradle and slumped back into his chair. His mother turned from the sink and sat with him. She didn't look angry anymore, just tired, as if the brief conversation with her ex-husband had taken the last bit of energy from her.

"Renny, I'm sorry about the trail cleanup project. I wish I could join you, but I have to host an open house that day." She stroked his hair gently.

Renny sighed. "That's okay, Mom. I know some other people who are doing the trail project, so I'll have fun anyway." He didn't add that he might be the only one without a parent there. In fact, that was the only reason he'd signed up in the first place — to spend some time with his dad. Now he'd just have to go by himself and hope someone else showed up alone.

8

It was funny, but his conversation with Turk hadn't made Bryce feel much better about things. He wasn't consumed by that burning fury anymore. A creeping guilt had taken its place. What would happen if Turk went overboard and really hurt Renny Harding? Bryce wondered. In a way, it would be his fault, wouldn't it? Turk's comment about "intensive care" was kind of scary.

Oh well, he consoled himself, it was too late to do anything about it now. He'd only told Turk to intimidate Renny — hadn't he? Or maybe he'd said to hit him with a few hard fouls. . . . He couldn't remember anymore.

"Bryce McCormack!"

Startled, Bryce came out of his reverie. His teacher, Ms. Hasselhof, was calling his name.

"Yes?" he asked, standing up.

"You're wanted in the office. Follow this young man."

"The office?" Bryce repeated dumbly.

"The principal's office," said Ms. Hasselhof meaningfully.

Bryce looked at the office monitor. It was Norm Harvey.

"Follow me," said Norm.

"I know the way," Bryce said, scowling as he brushed past Norm and out of math class. "What are you now, the principal's errand boy?"

"Office squad," Norm explained. "It's for extra credit. Something you wouldn't know anything about."

"Shut up, you stupid nerd!" Bryce said, grabbing the kid by the shirt.

"Uh-uh-uh!" Norm warned him off. "I think this is the kind of behavior the principal wants to talk to you about."

Uh-oh. Bryce suddenly realized what was hap-

46

pening. That stupid fight he'd had with Chris Brown last week. He'd thought everyone had forgotten about that one!

Sure enough, there was Chris, sitting on one of the chairs in the principal's outer office. He sneered at Bryce, but Bryce didn't react.

Principal O'Keefe came out, her secretary right behind her. "You two boys know why you're here. I have come up with a suitable punishment for you. Either you will sit in the school library for three hours and write an essay of one thousand words or more about 'Why Violence Is Wrong,' or you will serve on the trail cleanup Saturday, up on Pyramid Mountain."

"I'll take the essay," Chris Brown said quickly.

Bryce shot him a look. "I'll go on the trail cleanup," he said. Anything but sit for three hours at a desk in the school library, staring into Chris Brown's stupid face while writing an essay about why violence is wrong.

"Fine," said Ms. O'Keefe. "Here is an evaluation sheet for you, Bryce. Bring it back filled out and signed by the person in charge."

"Yes, Ms. O'Keefe," Bryce said.

This was going to be a real treat, Bryce thought disgustedly. He hated work. He hoped Chris Brown would get an F on his essay and have to do it all over again.

That weekend, Bryce showed up at Pyramid Mountain as directed. There was a crowd of kids and adults standing around the park headquarters. "Uh, hi, is this the trail cleaning detail?" Bryce asked the man who seemed to be in charge.

"Yes, it is, and you are . . . ?" the man asked with a pleasant smile.

"Bryce McCormack," Bryce said. "The, uh, principal sent me down to help." He cleared his throat, embarrassed, avoiding the curious glances of the kids, some of whom he knew.

"All right, Bryce," the man said. "I'm Mr. Sarlin, and this is the cleanup crew. Will your father or mother be joining you?"

Bryce shook his head slowly. No one had told him that this was a parent-kid event. Oh, brother, he thought, rolling his eyes. This is going to be worse than I thought.

"Hmmm," the man said, scratching his head. "Hey, everybody. Bryce is going to be helping us today. Is there someone who isn't paired with a cleaning buddy?"

No one answered. Apparently all the other kids had parents with them. That was fine with Bryce. He'd rather be alone, anyway. Then, once the cleanup began, he could find a nice place to hide until it was all over.

"Hey, Mr. Sarlin, I'm here!" The rear door of a car in the parking lot opened, and a thin boy came running toward them at blazing speed.

Hey, wait a minute. Bryce knew that kid — it was —

"Hiya, Renny! Glad you could make it," Mr. Sarlin said cheerfully. "Bryce, you're in luck — your trail buddy has just arrived!"

"Bryce?" Renny said, stopping short in surprise. "Hi! What are you doing here?"

"I'll tell you later," Bryce said. "Come on, let's get going." He was anxious to get away from the crowd of cheerful do-gooders.

At Mr. Sarlin's direction, all the pairs came up to get their rubber gloves, garbage bags, and hedge clippers. Then, two by two, they went off in different directions. Renny and Bryce stopped at the head of a trail marked "Swamp View."

Bryce grimaced. "Whoopee, this looks like fun," he said flatly.

Renny didn't seem to hear the sarcastic tone in his voice. "One of us has to do the picking and clipping, the other one holds the bag. Which do you want to do?" Renny asked him.

"Um, the bag, I guess," Bryce said, taking a super-strength garbage bag from Renny and flapping it open. Taking the bag was a no-brainer, Bryce thought, smiling to himself. The kid was a moron to even give him a choice. Renny was going to do all the bending and picking up of gross stuff. All Bryce had to do was hold the bag open.

"You sure you want the bag?" Renny asked dubiously.

"I'm sure," Bryce said firmly, closing the subject.

"Okay, then." Renny led the way down the trail. He began picking up litter and tossing it into Bryce's bag. Within minutes, the bag was half-full, stinking, and starting to get heavy. And they were just getting started!

"What do you say we take a break?" Bryce suggested.

"You tired already?" Renny asked, looking genuinely surprised. "We've barely begun."

"What do we do when our bag is full?" Bryce asked, hoping the answer would be "We're finished and we can go home."

It wasn't. "Well, when the bag is full, we tie it off and leave it at the head of the trail for the park rangers to pick up later," Renny replied. "Then we take another bag and start over, until the three hours is up."

"I should have done the essay," Bryce muttered. If he'd known he was going to get stuck with Renny Harding — the kid who had turned his dream into a nightmare — and holding a smelly bag of garbage for three hours, he would have done anything else, even faced suspension.

For the next hour, Renny picked up soda cans, paper cups, and other trash, tossed them into the bag, and attacked the weeds and saplings that threatened to choke off the trail. Bryce trailed behind him, surprised at how much the kid seemed to be enjoying himself. It made him feel a little embarrassed for his own sour attitude.

"I think it's time for a break," Bryce said when he'd tied off his third bag. "I'm breaking." Without waiting for Renny to agree, he put down the garbage bag and sat on a felled tree trunk.

Renny sat down next to Bryce and wiped his brow with his T-shirt. "Whoo — sweaty work," he said, grinning. "But it's all for a good cause, huh?"

"Right," Bryce said, nodding. Right — though he could care less about hikers or nature lovers.

"So you were going to tell me how you wound up doing this," Renny prompted him.

"Oh, yeah," Bryce said, stalling. For some reason, he didn't want to tell Renny the truth. "Well, I used to do this with my parents when I was little." Which was true. Bryce's mom had loved to volunteer the whole family for charity work. "My dad always hated it; he just wanted to stay home and watch the ball game. Maybe that's why he left home when I was in third grade."

"Hey — my folks are divorced, too!" Renny said, turning to stare at Bryce. "Just last year. That's how come my mom and I ended up moving here."

"Huh!" Bryce said, looking Renny in the eye for the first time. "I hate my dad. You?"

"I don't *hate* him," Renny replied slowly. "But I am kind of mad at him. We were supposed to work on this cleanup project together, but he couldn't make it at the last minute." Renny picked up a stray soda can and hurled it into the garbage bag with more force than he'd used before.

"Then your dad's a jerk, and so's mine." Bryce snorted. "I never see him except when he drops off Christmas presents. And then I make him sorry he did."

"You don't really *hate* him, do you?" Renny asked.

"Sure I do," Bryce insisted. "Why'd he have to leave?" He tore a stick off a nearby tree and started digging in the trail dirt with it.

"I don't know," Renny said. "I don't really get why my dad left, either. But I do know I still miss him."

Bryce felt a sick feeling welling up from the pit of his stomach. He clenched down hard on it. "I don't want to talk about it," he said tightly.

"Okay," Renny said, backing off.

The two boys were silent for a while, each brooding over his own thoughts.

"Well, I bet your dad is proud of you, even if you don't think so," Renny said finally. "You're good at so many sports — baseball, lacrosse, track, soccer. I saw you in the all-state basketball tournament. You were awesome!"

Bryce felt a distinct flush of pleasure. "Thanks," he said. "You saw that? That was way over in Chicasaw."

"I made my mom take me," Renny said. "I'm not good at basketball, but I love to watch it. And you were the best one there."

"I don't know about that. . . ."

"That flying spin move? How do you do that?"

"I do it in soccer, too," Bryce admitted with a sly smile. Suddenly the kid didn't seem so bad to him anymore. He was actually okay. And hey — it wasn't his fault he was a good player!

"No way!" Renny cried. "Airborne, or on the ground?"

"Sort of both," Bryce said, trying to explain how he did his patented move. He got up and demonstrated. "You wait for the defender to commit, see. Then, when he does, you just use his momentum and spin off him, depending on which way he goes. You cradle the ball between your legs, then let it go before you hit ground."

54

"Awesome." Renny shook his head in deep admiration. "I could never do that. Nobody but you could do it."

"Aw . . ."

"You know, ever since I moved here, I've wanted to play soccer like you."

"Really?" Bryce thought back to October. "Which team were you on in the fall?"

"I wasn't. I got here after the season started, and all the teams were set. I just came down every week and watched. Mostly your games, actually. I'd stand there, imagining myself as center striker. . . ." Renny laughed, remembering. "Funny, huh?"

"So that's why nobody knew about you," Bryce said. "Well, you've got nothing to be ashamed of. You play a good little game."

Renny beamed. "You know that day in Conroy's, when you came up to me and encouraged me?" he asked. "You were really nice about it. I mean, we beat you, but you didn't hold it against me or anything. I thought that was really cool."

Looking into Renny's open, honest face, Bryce felt a little twinge of guilt. He remembered that day in Conroy's, all right, when he had approached

Renny to see what he was all about — not to be "really nice." Thinking about that day reminded him of his conversation with Turk Walters and the malicious grin on Turk's face. The twinge of guilt turned into a much bigger pang.

"Hey, kid — I mean Renny," Bryce said suddenly.

"Yeah?" Renny asked. He must have sensed the importance of what Bryce was about to say, because he looked at him very seriously.

"I, uh, you know the game tomorrow?" Bryce shifted uncomfortably on the log. "Well, I heard a, um, a rumor —"

Renny held up his hand. "I bet I heard the same rumor — that Coach Harrelson is going to be there to check out the players, right?" He grinned at Bryce. "You know, I overheard him talking about you last week. He couldn't believe how good you were. You're a shoo-in for the starting spot on junior varsity next year."

Bryce stared at Renny. Coach Harrelson had said something that made Renny think he wanted him, Bryce, to be his center striker! But the coach had also said good — no, make that great — things about Renny's playing. Had Coach Harrelson made up his mind yet? He had at least one more game to watch Renny. But if the Blue Hornets beat the Orange Crush tomorrow, then it would be Bryce's Yellow Jackets against Renny's Blue Hornets in the best-of-three championship series. Coach Harrelson would see Renny play not once, but at least three more times.

Until recently, Bryce wouldn't have worried about his competition. But now, he wasn't so sure he'd come out on top when compared to Renny. The thought burned him.

"So was I right, was that the rumor you heard?" Renny asked. "Or was there something else you wanted to tell me?"

Bryce knew he should warn Renny about Turk. He knew that Renny might even get hurt if he didn't. But the thought of having to face Renny in the championships made him choke on the warning. He couldn't get the words out — he just couldn't.

Renny was still looking at him, waiting.

Bryce forced himself to say something. "Yeah, that was the rumor, all right. But, um, do you mind a little advice? In the game, try to be a little more aggressive, you know? You've got to throw yourself at the ball more. I mean, I know you're not big like me, but you still have to act like it sometimes, or — or kids on the other team might try to push you around, intimidate you. Know what I mean?"

There, Bryce thought. If the kid can't take a hint, too bad. That's as much warning as he's going to get.

"You're saying I should play more like you?" Renny asked with a grin. "Gee, it would be great if I could! Wanna go out there and pretend to be me?"

Bryce tried to laugh along, but it wasn't easy. "Really, try to be a little more selfish, too — I mean, if you've got the shot, take the shot. Otherwise, they'll figure out you're going to pass off every time and start covering you better. Gotta keep surprising them, doing the unexpected."

"Well, I guess you're right. I guess I'm a little scared to get hurt sometimes. Some of the kids are so much bigger than me."

Bryce thought of Turk Walters again and swallowed hard. Even though he didn't want Renny's team to win, he sure hoped the kid got through tomorrow's game without getting hurt.

"Well, we'd better get back to work," Renny said, getting up. "Thanks for the advice." He suddenly stuck out his hand. "I feel like we're friends now, sort of."

"Sure," Bryce agreed, tossing it off. He managed to shake Renny's hand, but he couldn't bring himself to look the kid in the eye.

"Come on," he said, flapping open his new garbage bag. "Let's get busy."

Renny had practice later that Saturday afternoon. He came all psyched up to play. Becoming friends with Bryce McCormack was so cool — someone who was into sports as much as Renny was, and a great athlete, too! Well, maybe they weren't really friends yet, but Bryce had given him all those good tips, and Renny was eager to try them out in practice. So it bothered him when he noticed that his teammates seemed to be acting down in the dumps. They were only half trying during the first set of drills, and no one was saying much of anything.

Renny couldn't understand it — they'd been playing so well. And now they were just one victory from the play-offs! Why should any of them be down?

He wondered what could be bothering them. So

during a break, he leaned against one of the goal-posts, listening to some of his teammates talking.

"The Orange Crush are dirty players," said Chuck Mathes, the team's goalie. "Last time we played them, Turk Walters kept crashing into me on purpose when the refs weren't looking. I finally complained to the ref, and he stopped doing it, but only because he knew he couldn't get away with it."

"What did they beat us by?" Jordan Woo asked.

"Seven to two. And that was when we had Isaac," Chuck replied.

"We better hope for a miracle," Jordan said. "How's Isaac's ankle?"

"Forget it. Anyway, Renny's doing just as well, or better even."

"Yeah, but Renny might be a fluke. What's it been, two games? He was a sub all season — just like me."

Good old Jordan, Renny thought sourly. Always good for a dark comment.

"Anyway, what's the use in talking about it?" Jordan continued. "We're going to get crushed by the Crush, unless a miracle happens."

Renny tossed his paper cup into the trash bag and turned to the two boys. "You know, you guys are already whipped," he said. "Just because they beat us once, and they're bigger than us, doesn't mean we can't win. We have to win! Otherwise, we're out of the play-offs!"

"Duh," Jordan said. "And your point is?"

"My point is, we've got to believe we can win, or we can't!" Renny said hotly. "We've got to make them scared of us, instead of the other way around."

"Oh, right." Chuck snorted. "How do you suggest we do that? Have you seen them? They look like college kids!"

"Well, for one thing, we use our speed advantage. If we stay far away from each other and use long passes, keep them in one-on-one situations, they'll have a hard time keeping up."

"Yeah, and when they start fouling us?" Henry Wilkes asked. The midfielder had come up to them in midconversation and now spoke up for the first time.

"Do some acting, fall down and scream and grab your arm — draw the foul!" Renny said.

Henry and Chuck looked at each other and grinned. "Hey, you know what? That's pretty cool," Henry said.

"And there are other things we can do," Renny said, warming to his subject.

"Like what?" Chuck asked, interested now.

"Like, we can force them to play in their own end."

"Yeah?"

"Sure — what if, first thing, we kicked the ball way down in their end, then put pressure on them, using our speed advantage? Every time we get the ball, just kick it as far as we can toward their goal, then rush the ball, try to rattle them?"

"It's risky," Henry pointed out. "We could get caught out of position."

"Let's just try it once, to start the game, okay?" Renny suggested.

"Shouldn't we ask Coach McMaster?" Jordan wondered. Suddenly it was his plan, too, Renny noticed.

"I'll run it by him," Renny agreed. "But you guys — you've got to think positive, okay? Let's keep the Crush off balance from the opening whistle. Like you already said, we can't beat them playing our usual way — and we've got to beat them, one way or another!"

Henry and Chuck looked at each other, then nodded. They bumped fists with Renny on it. Even Jordan Woo stuck his hand in.

"And don't let me hear any more whipped-dog talk!" Renny said.

"Okay, Captain," Henry said with a grin. "Crush the Crush!"

"Yeah!" Chuck said.

"All right!" Renny said, and ran off to talk to the coach about his idea.

Captain. Henry had called him captain. Of course, he wasn't really team captain, Isaac Mendez was. But for the past two games, he'd been the team scoring leader, its spark plug, keeping them in the play-off hunt in spite of the real captain's injury. It was fine with Renny if they wanted to call him captain.

Where was Coach McMaster, anyway? Renny looked around and spotted him at the other end of the field with some other players. Renny ran toward them.

All of a sudden, a hulking red-haired figure stepped out from behind a tree by the side of the field. "Harding!"

It was Turk Walters, the kid on the Orange Crush who had smacked into Chuck Mathes the last time the two teams played each other. Renny didn't like the look of this at all. What did Turk want with him?

Renny decided to keep going. "Hi, Turk," he said as he went by. "Can't talk now."

"Yo, Harding, I'm talking to you!" Turk yelled, grabbing Renny by the shoulder and spinning him around to face him.

"Look, I'm in the middle of practice," Renny said, trying not to panic. "What do you want?"

"I only need a minute," Turk said with a smile. "I just wanted to let you know — tomorrow, you're dead meat." He held tightly on to Renny's shoulder, squeezing a little.

Renny winced. "W-what do you mean?" he asked, his voice quivering a little.

"I hear you're the new big man on the Blue Hornets. And it's my job to cut big men down to size, okay?"

Renny winced again as Turk's grip grew even tighter.

"You better be prepared to get slammed around,"

Turk said. "Because if you come my way, I'm gonna stop you stone cold."

"Long as you play fair," Renny said, trying in vain to pull away.

"Fair?" Turk smiled, even laughed a little to himself. "Yeah, I heard of that. It rhymes with *square*. See you tomorrow, punk. You better be ready." With a shove, Turk released Renny and moved off into the shadow of the trees.

Renny watched him disappear. He was shaking with anger and fear. Should he tell Coach McMaster what Turk had just said? No, then the coach might pull Renny from center striker position just to avoid any possible trouble. Renny decided to say nothing.

He went over to where his stuff was, at the side of the field. He gathered it all up, then started to walk home. Coach and the others would wonder why he'd left early, but Renny didn't care. All the energy had been drained out of him by his encounter with Turk Walters. Suddenly, he was even more afraid of the Orange Crush than his teammates had been.

Come on, suck it up! he told himself, still shaking all over. He's not gonna really do anything.

Yet deep inside, Renny wasn't so sure. Turk had a reputation for playing rough, and he'd come right out and threatened Renny.

Renny told himself not to back down. He just hoped that when the time came, he'd have the courage to stand his ground under fire. That's what Bryce McCormack would do, he reminded himself.

10

Bryce didn't need an alarm clock to wake up the next morning. He was up at eight sharp and out of the house by nine. His mother hadn't even woken up yet, so he rode his bike down to the dew-covered field, drawn there as if by a magnetic force.

Renny Harding was playing at nine-thirty. So was Turk Walters. And Bryce had finally made up his mind to do something about it.

He liked the kid, he realized now. Sure, Renny was kind of naive and innocent, but he was also genuinely nice. Besides, Renny's dad had left the family, just like his own father had. And though Bryce's father had been gone for years and years, Renny's had left only recently. That poor kid. Bryce knew how he must feel.

No. He had to do something for Renny. He

couldn't admit to having schemed against him, but there was somebody else he could be straight with, and Bryce now sought him out on the sidelines.

It was ten minutes till game time, and Turk Walters was loosening up, banging into a tree for practice.

"Doesn't that hurt?" Bryce asked him by way of saying hi.

"Soccer's a contact sport; didn't anybody ever tell you that?" Turk shot back. "Hey, man, I've gotta thank you for the advice. I already tested it out on that kid, and he's shakin' in his cleats, believe me."

"Uh, yeah, about that . . ." Bryce said. "Listen, I was wrong about that kid."

"Huh?" Turk stopped banging the tree and turned to pay closer attention to Bryce.

"I don't think it's a good idea to actually foul him. Just scaring him's much better. That way, the Hornets don't get any free kicks or anything."

Turk snorted. "Don't worry," he said with a laugh. "I'm not gonna get caught. I'm gonna hit him when the refs aren't looking — when he hasn't got the ball."

"Yeah, but I still don't think —"

"Hey, you know what?" Turk said, taking a step toward Bryce. "Enough already. Just shut up now and let me do the dirty work."

"Don't hurt him, Turk," Bryce said, holding his ground.

"Aw, poor Bryce, his heart is bleeding for the kid," Turk taunted him. "So now you want me to forget the whole thing, huh?"

"That's right," Bryce said. "It's a bad idea, Turk. Let it rest, okay?"

"Oh. Okay. So why don't I go tell the kid it was you who gave me the bright idea? That would be 'right,' wouldn't it?"

Bryce went cold. Turk laughed.

"Go take a seat and watch the show," Turk said. "It's gonna be real physical. And you'd better keep your mouth shut, understand?"

Bryce backed away. He headed for the wooden bleachers where the parents sat, feeling lower than a worm. If Renny got hurt, he'd never forgive himself.

On the other hand, what more could he have done? He'd tried to talk Turk out of it, but it was no use! The damage had already been done, hadn't it? It's too late to fix things now, Bryce told himself.

Watching the teams line up for the start of the game, Bryce smiled sadly. He had been worried about facing Renny Harding in the play-offs, but now he could relax. That wasn't going to happen. Bryce's nasty trick had worked, and now the Yellow Jackets would be facing the Orange Crush in the play-offs instead of the Blue Hornets.

Turk's team would be a pushover, Bryce thought, trying to make himself feel better. With Renny Harding out of the way, I'm sure to get the MVP trophy. And Coach Harrelson will be there to watch, so I'll have another chance to impress him — this time without Renny Harding around to spoil everything.

On the surface, things were working out just right. So why did he feel so miserable about it? Why couldn't he shake off this horrible guilty feeling?

The whistle blew, and Bryce looked up. The game had begun. Good. A chance to forget his troubles for a while.

Just so long as Turk didn't hurt the kid . . .

11

Renny was riding high. His plan for an all-out rush into the Crush zone right at the opening whistle had paid off, big-time. The Crush defenders were taken off guard, faced with a five-man rush before they'd even gotten set. The result was an easy goal by Renny and a 1–0 lead before the first minute of the game was past.

"Now we go back to our normal set," Renny told his fellow frontliners. "Hold your positions. But just keep kicking it downfield every time. We have to keep the play in their end!"

The whistle blew and play resumed, with the Orange Crush advancing with the ball. Knowing that a long kick was coming the moment one of the Blue Hornets got a foot on it, Renny snuck downfield, behind the Crush attack but just outside the Crush zone, so he wouldn't be called offside. There. Any minute now . . .

"Ooof!" Suddenly Renny went flying through the air, hit by what felt like a battering ram. He landed with a thud, banging his left knee against the hard, dry turf. He got up slowly and looked around to see Turk Walters retreating back into his own zone.

Renny tried to put some weight on the knee. It hurt, and he limped around, trying to walk off the blow. He waved to the ref for a whistle, but the ref didn't see him. He called to the coach to take him out.

"Gotta get a whistle first!" Coach McMaster called back. "You okay?"

Renny shook his head, then tried to run over to the sideline so he could get out of the way of the on-coming rush.

"Injury time-out!" Coach McMaster yelled as the ref ran past. The ref blew his whistle, and Renny limped across the line, then flopped to the ground.

His knee was bleeding, but it didn't look too bad. From the receding pain, Renny sensed that he'd be okay in a minute or so, and that was what he told the coach. "I got fouled," he said. "But I'm okay."

"Okay, I'll get you back in there," the coach said. "Meanwhile, clean that off and get a bandage on it. Here's the first aid kit."

Renny did as he was told. He ripped open a cleansing pad and washed the cut, then covered it with a large padded bandage. Finishing the job, he glanced up at the bleachers. There, among the parents and other spectators, sat Bryce McCormack.

Bryce had his chin in his hands, so that his mouth was covered. He was looking right at Renny with horrified eyes. Renny waved to him, letting Bryce know he was okay. But Bryce didn't acknowledge him. He just sat there staring, with that weird look on his face.

A roar went up from the other side of the field. "Oh, no!" Jordan Woo moaned. "Curt Kelly scored a goal for them — he just mowed our defense right down! Man, we're gonna lose now for sure. These guys are just too big for us."

Renny didn't take the time to dignify Jordan's comment with a rebuke. Instead, he swung around toward where the coach was standing. "I'm back in!" he shouted.

"Substitution, ref!" the coach yelled, then waved Renny onto the field. "Cooper, take a rest!" he called, motioning for Ellis Cooper, one of the defensemen, to come out.

"Coach, let me in at center striker!" Renny protested. "They're just trying to intimidate me!"

"Let's see how you move around first," the coach replied. "I don't want you getting hurt."

Renny kicked the dirt in frustration, then trotted onto the field, refusing to let his pain show. There was no limp in his step. He glared across at Turk Walters, but Turk wasn't looking at him.

Play resumed, and Renny stayed back on defense, waiting for the action to flow his way. After a couple of missed shots, the ball was kicked out by the Crush's goalie, and now half a dozen players were headed right for Renny, with the ball up for grabs.

Renny rushed out to kick it back the other way. He got there well before the onrushing players and laced into it, sending it toward the Crush goal.

Renny stopped, and most of the other players turned around to follow the play. But one kept coming. Before Renny could brace himself, Turk Walters banged into him again. Renny was blasted backward by the blow. The back of his head thudded hard against the ground.

Again, there was no whistle. The referee, following the play, had missed this foul, just as he'd missed the last one.

Renny wanted to go over to the ref and complain. But that would just make Turk Walters think he was a wimp. No, Renny decided. He would take his revenge on the field!

Abandoning his position, Renny ran forward to midfield and took control of the loose ball. Forgetting that he was supposed to be playing defense, he scooted forward with the ball right down the middle of the field. He outran everyone but two defenders, who stood their ground in front of him. One was Turk Walters.

"Come on, punk, come on," Turk beckoned him. "Try getting by me."

Renny kept coming. At the last moment, Turk rushed forward, yelling at the top of his lungs.

Normally, Renny would have deked him and kept on going, shifting directions just enough to make Turk fall all over himself.

But what Renny hadn't realized was just how much Turk had scared him with his threats the previous day — and with the first two dirty hits he'd laid on him today. With Turk coming at him, screaming, Renny froze, then panicked. He kicked the ball away and ducked to his left, curling over to avoid getting hit.

Turk stopped just short of him, then laughed. "Chicken!" he said.

Renny looked to see what had happened to the ball. It was being rushed back upfield by the Crush — right past his own abandoned defensive position!

In no time, the goal was scored and it was 2–1 in favor of the Crush. "Good going, punk!" Turk said. "You just cost your team a goal!" He laughed nastily. Renny heard it as he trotted back to his own sideline.

"Coach, I —"

"Sit down and take a rest, Renny," Coach Mc-Master said. "You were supposed to be playing defense — what happened? Who told you to play center striker? And if you're gonna do that, at least take the shot! Don't pass it away to somebody who isn't there!"

Coach had never talked to him like this before. Truth was, he hadn't had to, Renny realized.

"You looked like you were afraid to get hit again," the coach said. "You can't play afraid, Renny — this is a contact sport."

"He was fouling me, Coach!" Renny protested. "Twice he hit me when nobody was looking. That's how I hurt the knee!"

The coach looked back at him soberly. "You're saying he hurt you deliberately?"

"Uh-huh."

"Which kid?"

"Number Eight," Renny said. "Turk Walters."

"I'll say something to the ref at halftime," the coach said. "Meanwhile, rest that knee. I'll put you in for the second half."

"But I need to get back in there —"

Just then, another roar came from across the field as the Crush scored yet again.

"Three–one. We're dead," Jordan Woo said. "We are such toast."

"Shut up, Jordan!" Renny said, irritated more at himself than his teammate. "We've still got time to come back. You've got to believe, Jordan! You've got to believe!"

Halftime came and went. The boys downed sports drinks, caught their breath, and gathered around their coach.

"Look, just keep hanging in there," Coach Mc-Master told his team. "We're only down by two goals. We're going to try to find Renny one on one, okay? I spoke to the ref just now about the boy who's been fouling him. We're going to see if we can get a call, maybe get a penalty shot. You okay with that, Renny?"

"You bet, Coach," Renny said.

He'd been thinking about what Bryce McCormack had told him out on the trail the day before. "Be a little more aggressive," he'd said, "or the other team might try to intimidate you."

Well, they'd succeeded, Renny had to admit. But the game wasn't over yet. Remembering what Bryce had told him about doing the unexpected, Renny made up his mind to take the shot if he had it, since the Crush had to be thinking he was scared of getting hit.

"Try to be more selfish," Bryce had told him. "Gotta keep surprising them."

Yes, he was going to be more selfish this half. Coach had set up the play for him, and if Turk hit him now, everyone would be watching.

He looked up at the bleachers. Bryce was gone.

Oh well, Renny thought. It was nice of him to watch part of my game, anyway.

He ran out onto the field as fast as he could, getting a loud cheer from his psyched-up teammates as they followed him.

As soon as the Hornets got control of the ball, they set up to feed Renny in the offensive zone. Turk Walters watched and waited, muttering so Renny could hear him, "Come on, punk, come on, I've got you. . . ."

The ball came to Renny. He dribbled toward Turk, who rushed at him again, yelling like a banshee.

Renny kept charging. At the last minute, he grabbed the ball between his shins, at the same time executing Bryce's "flying spin" move. He'd tried it out in the driveway before heading for the field that morning. The move worked — as he came out of the spin, he was almost past the startled Turk. Instinctively, though, at the last instant, Turk stuck out his foot and tripped Renny. It was nothing compared to the fouls he'd committed in the first half. But this time, the ref — and everyone else — was watching.

Renny fell, and the ball spun free. The whistle blew harshly. Turk jumped up into the air, yelling as if he were in pain. "No!" he said. "It was a clean hit!"

"Penalty shot!" the ref said. "Flagrant foul in the zone!"

"Let me take the shot!" Renny said to his teammates.

"I've got a stronger shot," John Singleman pointed out.

"I'm taking it," Renny insisted. "I'm the one who got fouled, and I'm going to put it in!"

Without waiting for an argument, Renny raised his hand and went over to where the ref had placed the ball. He backed up a few paces, measuring them off carefully. Then he sized up the goalie and took a deep breath.

Renny ran at the ball and reared his foot back to kick. At that split second, the goalie leaned to his left ever so slightly. That was the direction Renny had been planning to kick the ball. In midkick, he diverted his foot just a little, so that the ball glanced off the side of his foot, near the little toe. The goalie, prone on the ground after a fruitless leap to stop a kick that never came, watched the ball trickle in behind him. The Hornets leaped into the air, screaming their heads off.

"Lucky shot!" some of the Crush called out. "He muffed it!"

Renny turned to them. "Nothing lucky about it," he said, before high-fiving his teammates.

Less than a minute later, Renny was at it again, leading a rush right through all three defensemen. Renny's shot hit the post but caromed right back to John Singleman, who shot it home. The score was tied 3–3, all thanks to Renny's new "selfishness."

A few minutes later, after an attack by the Crush had been turned back, Renny found himself up against Turk again. He put his body between Turk and the ball, cradling it, pushing back against Turk to make him give ground.

That got Turk's temper up, as Renny had hoped it would. The big defenseman gave Renny a hard shove. "Get off me!" he yelled.

The ref's whistle blew. "Number Eight, Orange —

that's your second flagrant foul. You're out of the game!"

"What!" Turk exploded. "He hit me first!"

The ref blew his whistle again and pointed toward the sidelines. Turk backed off, still staring furiously at Renny.

Let him steam, Renny thought happily. He can't touch me now.

With very little time left and the score still tied, Renny knew that Turk's ejection had given him the chance he'd been waiting for. Getting to the ball, he kicked it as far as he could toward the Crush zone, then ran for all he was worth to catch up to it.

John Singleman was already there, trying to get around the defense. Renny got free and called for the ball. John passed it to him.

All second half, whenever he'd gotten the ball in the zone, Renny had taken the shot. Now, when the Crush rushed up to deny him, he remembered Bryce's advice to keep them off balance. Renny lifted the ball with his foot and headed it over the defenders, right to Brian Cardone, who was on the right wing.

Brian quickly turned and shot. The ball went just

past the goalie's outstretched hand and into the net. At that very moment, the ref's whistle blew three times, signaling the end of the game. The Blue Hornets had won!

The whole team went wild. "We're in the play-offs! We're in the play-offs!" Jordan Woo kept saying. "I knew we could do it! You've got to believe!"

Renny had to laugh as his teammates hoisted Brian skyward to put him on their shoulders. Jordan had been the biggest pessimist on the whole team. Arguing hadn't convinced him — only Renny's brilliant play on the field had made a believer out of Jordan.

So why should I hold it against him? Renny thought. We're in now — and no matter what happens from here on in, nobody can take that away from us. Not ever.

12

By the middle of the first half, Bryce had had enough. He couldn't stand to see Renny beaten up any more. So he'd headed for Conroy's, where he knew the winning team would soon show up.

As he sat there, sipping a glass of milk and picking at a plate of fries, he thought of Renny getting stomped into mush by Turk Walters. It was all his fault, Bryce knew. He had done something awful, and his punishment would be the gift of getting the Orange Crush as a play-off opponent.

He wondered what Turk would say when he walked in. Bryce could picture the big, mean grin he'd be wearing. He hated Turk Walters almost as much as he hated himself at that moment.

But it wasn't Turk who burst through the doorway with a big smile on his face. It was Renny Harding!

Renny came in yelling, "We did it!" at the top of his lungs, followed by ten other Blue Hornets, all high-fiving and whooping it up.

Bryce sat there, frozen. He was totally unprepared for this unexpected turn of events. Unbelievably, the Blue Hornets had won!

Renny saw him and came up to him. "Guess what?" he told Bryce, putting an arm around his shoulders. "We beat the Crush, four–three!"

"Hey, all right," Bryce said with a weak smile and a little nod. "Good for you."

He looked at Renny to see if he could spot any major wounds. But no, there was nothing . . . a little limp, maybe, but certainly nothing like Bryce was afraid would be there.

"I'm glad you're okay," he told Renny truthfully. "I saw you get hit a couple of times."

"Awww," Renny said with a warm smile. "I'm okay. That kid Turk is really a dirty player! He was purposely trying to hurt me."

"Yeah . . ." Bryce mumbled, looking away.

"He had me messed up for a while there," Renny confessed. "I was starting to shy away from the action. But then I thought of what you told me."

"Me?" Bryce turned to look at Renny again.

"'Don't let them intimidate you,' you said," Renny reminded him. "You were my inspiration out there today." He clapped Bryce on the back. "So now we get to face off in the championship series. It's going to be so cool! Two out of three, Blue Hornets and Yellow Jackets, for the title. I can't wait."

"Me neither," Bryce said, his mood darkening.

You and your big mouth, a voice inside his head said. First you set Turk after him — who probably would have gone after him anyhow — then you give Renny the piece of advice that helps him win! Now his team's in the championships. How are you going to feel if he outplays you and walks off with the MVP trophy? Who's Coach Harrelson going to be impressed with then, huh? You stupid loser!

Bryce winced and tried to shut out the little voice.

"Got a headache?" Renny asked. "What's the matter, aren't you feeling well? You haven't even touched your fries."

"What are you, my mother?" Bryce asked sharply. Then he pulled back, seeing the hurt look in Renny's eyes. After all, Renny was a good kid. He hadn't done anything bad to Bryce, other than play good soccer. It wasn't as if he'd purposely shown him up or anything like that. "Sorry," he managed to say.

"Anyway, thanks again for the advice," Renny said. "It sure did the trick today. See you at the championship!" He went to join his teammates.

Bryce nodded. "Yeah," he muttered under his breath. "And this time, I'll know you're coming."

Bryce paid for his uneaten fries and left the store, still torn about everything that had happened.

"Hey, McCormack!"

Bryce came to a sudden stop as Turk Walters loomed up in front of him, scowling. "Oh, hey, Turk," Bryce said. "I heard you lost. Too bad."

"Yeah, too bad," Turk said darkly. "Too bad for you, you double-crossing bum!"

"What are you talking about?" Bryce asked, annoyed.

"That was some great 'advice' you gave me," Turk said. "You lost us the game, jerk!"

"Oh, yeah? How'd I do that?" Bryce asked, not giving an inch.

"Your advice got me kicked out, that's how!" Turk shouted. "First it gave them a penalty shot, which that kid Renny converted, by the way. Then I had to watch from the sidelines while they scored the winning goal. You think they would have scored if I'd been out there?"

"I don't know. Probably," Bryce said. "That kid Renny's good. Besides, I didn't tell you to foul him *dirty*. You did that on your own. Face it — you should have listened to me when I told you to forget the whole thing."

For a minute, Turk looked as if he were going to haul off and take a swing at Bryce. But evidently he decided Bryce was too tough. "I'm gonna get that kid," he growled, kicking the dirt.

"You'd better leave him alone," Bryce said.

"What are you, his protector or something?" Turk wanted to know.

"He's a good kid," Bryce said. "You leave him alone or I'm going to have something to say about it, you hear me?"

Turk's eyes narrowed as he stared back at Bryce. He nodded menacingly, then walked right past Bryce, muttering, "I hear you, McCormack. I hear you, all right."

Bryce looked after him, shaking his head. Turk's a real loser, he thought. Renny Harding has a hundred times more going for him.

Bryce thought about the upcoming championship series. Only one team would come out the winner. He and Renny might never meet head on, because they'd both be playing on the front line, but it would still be a contest between the two of them. Each was his team's best player, the one the team looked to when a crucial score was needed.

There would be only one MVP. Coach Harrelson would be watching every game, and he would remember how each boy played when it came time to select the JV team's center striker next fall.

Bryce wasn't worried or scared, just determined. He walked up his front steps, smiling. This was going to be interesting. May the best man win, he said to himself.

13

The two-out-of-three championship round was scheduled tightly, with games on Friday afternoon, Saturday at noon, and Sunday at noon if necessary. It was almost Memorial Day weekend, and baseball season had begun. Space on the field was scarce.

Renny was driven to the first game of the series by his mom, on her way to show some houses to potential buyers. Renny got out of the car and ran to join his teammates. He had never been so excited in his entire life! He couldn't wait to go up against the mighty Yellow Jackets. He knew Bryce was going to score his share of goals this series, but Renny was determined to do the same for his team. Bryce had inspired him to take the leadership role on the Hornets.

He wasn't worried that Bryce would hate him if

the Hornets won, either. Renny felt sure that he and Bryce were friends now. That was the best part about this championship series. The only thing better would have been if he and Bryce were on the same team.

Suddenly, Turk Walters was standing opposite him. "Hey, Harding," he said. "I've got to talk to you."

"What do you want?" Renny asked sharply. He had no desire to talk to Turk, unless Turk wanted to apologize for trying to hurt him.

"C'mere," Turk urged, waving for him to come closer.

Reluctantly, Renny did so. "I've got to warm up," he said impatiently. "Make it fast."

"I just wanted you to know," Turk said with a mean little smile, "that it wasn't my idea to rough you up."

"Who told you to do it? Your coach?" Renny asked disbelievingly.

"No," Turk said. "As a matter of fact, it was Bryce McCormack."

Renny looked at Turk, dumbfounded. "Get out of here; I don't believe you."

"Why? You two such good buddies?" Turk prodded.

"We get along okay," Renny shot back. "He wouldn't do something like that."

"Oh, no?" Turk asked, the mean little smile returning. "Why don't you ask him, then? Watch his eyes. You'll see." Turk took a few steps away, then turned back to Renny. "The eyes don't lie, Harding. Oh, and hey, for what it's worth — I hope you kick the pants off those guys."

As Renny watched Turk lumber off, he felt suddenly sick to his stomach. Could it really be true? Bryce had been so nice to him, so friendly — had it all been a big lie? Had Bryce really played him like that?

Just before the game, Bryce approached Renny, hand extended. "Hey, good game, okay?" he said with a warm smile.

Renny stared back at him coldly. "Did you tell Turk Walters to come after me?" he asked, staring into Bryce's eyes.

The eyes flickered in panic for just a split second.

"Uh, no!" Bryce said, a little too hotly. "Did he tell you that?"

"You did, didn't you." It wasn't a question, it was a statement.

Bryce cleared his throat. "I was just discussing strategy with him, that's all. Hey, I never thought he'd try to hurt you."

"Uh-huh," Renny said. He sneered at Bryce's still-outstretched hand. Bryce lowered it. "See you on the field, Bryce," he said. He turned his back on Bryce and ran off toward the Hornets' bench, a white-hot coal of anger and hurt burning in his stomach.

When the whistle blew minutes later to start the game, Renny was everywhere. He reached the ball before anyone else could, constantly a step ahead of all the other players. And his shots, when he took them, were much more powerful than usual. Before ten minutes had passed, he had already scored two goals and just missed on a third.

After each goal, Renny looked over at Bryce and caught his eye. Then he pointed straight at him, as if to say, "In your face."

Bryce stared back at him, and Renny could see

that he was angry, too. But Renny didn't care. He was on a rampage, and nothing was going to stop him until he'd rubbed Bryce's face in it for betraying him like that!

After the second goal, Bryce controlled the ball for the Yellow Jackets, driving the play into the Hornets' zone. Renny saw an opportunity and sneaked up on Bryce from behind, diving and spearing the ball with his foot.

Bryce lost control of the ball, and it went straight to Jordan Woo, who was playing some of his rare minutes on defense. Jordan wound up and kicked it hard. For once, he hit the ball square, and it floated over everyone's heads back downfield. Renny was right behind it, racing to take possession. He ran the length of the field, bearing down on the goalie.

Only one defender stood in his way. Renny froze him with a fake to the left, then went around his right side, unimpeded. He kicked the ball straight up to the height of his head, then made as if to head the ball into the goal. Out of the corner of his eye he saw the goalie commit himself to the left — so when the ball hit the ground in front of his foot, Renny kicked it to the right side of the net.

The stunned goalie never had a chance. Renny could hear the roar of approval, and it was coming from both sides of the field. As he trotted back toward the center line, he gave a little wave of acknowledgment. They were cheering for *him!*

His anger drained right out of him, replaced by a deep sense of satisfaction. Bryce had betrayed him, but he'd also been Renny's inspiration. And now Renny was getting his revenge, in the best possible way.

14

At first, when Renny had accused him, Bryce felt guilty. When Renny had scored his first goal, Bryce figured it was only right, considering. Even the pointing didn't bother him — much. But when Renny had shown him up like that, stealing the ball from him and going all the way with it, Bryce had had enough.

The score was 3–0 already. But there was still another half to play. "We just have to be patient," Bryce told his teammates, "and wait for our opportunities. Follow me into their zone. I'll try to create something."

When the second half began, Bryce went out to the center circle expecting to see Renny facing him down. But Renny was not there — it was John Singleman instead. So where was Renny?

Bryce looked around for him. There he was, with the midfielders. What was going on? he wondered.

Bryce soon found out. Apparently, Renny had convinced his coach that with a three-goal lead, he should be put in as a midfielder to shadow Bryce wherever he went. For the first ten minutes of the half, every time the ball came to Bryce, Renny was there, harassing him, denying him possession or a clear lane. The only thing Bryce could do was to pass the ball away under the ferocious pressure.

Bryce could see that if this kept up, the game would end with the score just as it was. I've got to break out of this! he told himself.

He knew that if he succeeded in getting deep into the Hornets' zone, Renny would have to abandon position to follow him. That would leave one of the Yellow Jackets' midfielders unguarded.

Bryce took the ball and forced it forward, trying to run around Renny. But Renny, with his speed, kept cutting Bryce off. Finally, Bryce had had enough. He gave Renny a sharp shove with his forearm, creating some elbowroom between them.

The way to the Hornets' zone was open. But before Bryce could take advantage of the opportunity, the ref's whistle blew, and he pointed to Bryce, indicating a foul.

"What?!" Bryce leaped into the air in sheer frustration. "He was all over me, ref!"

The ref just shook his head. "Flagrant personal foul!" he said. "Free kick, Blue!"

"Nooooo!" Bryce yelled, banging his knees in frustration.

Eric Dornquist tapped him on the shoulder. "You're out, Bryce," he said. "I'm in for you."

Bryce looked up, then over at the sideline. Coach Hickey was motioning him off the field! Bryce couldn't believe it.

He walked slowly toward the sideline. "Come on, come on!" the coach urged him. "Hustle, Bryce! What's the matter with you?"

"He set me up for that foul, Coach," Bryce complained.

"And you fell for it," Coach Hickey replied, shaking his head. "If you'd stop hogging the ball for once and get your teammates into the flow, this stuff wouldn't happen."

They both turned their attention to the field, where Renny's free kick had turned into another goal, this time scored by Henry Wilkes. "Four–zip," the coach said sadly. "I can't believe this!"

Neither could Bryce. The first game was shaping up to be a first-class nightmare — all because Renny had found out the truth about him and Turk Walters.

"Did you see that shot he took in the first half?"

Bryce knew that voice. He turned to see Coach Harrelson talking with another man. Both of them had notepads and pens. They were looking out on the field, where Renny Harding was dancing around with the ball again.

"I thought you said he had a weak shot," the other man said.

"Guess I was wrong," Coach Harrelson said. "Or else he's just getting better with age."

The two men laughed, and Bryce felt tears filling his eyes. He sank down on the bench and turned away from them.

A minute later, defenseman Steve Weintraub came out of the game and sat down with him. "This really stinks," he said to Bryce.

"Tell me about it. Say, who's the guy with Coach Harrelson?" Bryce asked.

"Don't you know him?" Steve asked. "That's

Coach Johnson — he runs the high school varsity team."

"Oh, great," Bryce said. "Just great." Just when he thought things couldn't get any worse.

It was a mercy when the final whistle blew. No other goals had been scored, but the first game of the championship had been a massacre all the way.

The kid had drawn first blood. Bryce sat there steaming, thinking not about the past, but about the future. I'm not through yet, he swore to himself. It's not over till it's over, Renny Harding.

15

Renny couldn't sleep. Today's game had been incredible. In fact, the whole last two-plus weeks had been like something out of a dream. He'd become the soccer sensation of the whole town — even Norm Harvey had called to congratulate him.

"You appear to have an excellent probability of winning the championship at this point," he had said. "In fact, the odds are three to one in your favor. And your stats would appear to put you in line for the play-off's Most Valuable Player!"

"Hey, it was only one game," Renny pointed out.

"But you've got momentum on your side," Norm said. "The psychological edge. Fascinating. It's a lot like chess, actually."

"Hey!" Renny said with a laugh. "That's my line!"

Norm had also mentioned that the high school

coaches had been there. He heard they'd been very impressed with Renny.

So now Renny lay awake, thinking about the possibilities. Maybe someday he'd play center striker in high school. Probably not, though. After all, Isaac Mendez and Bryce were both bigger and stronger than he was, and almost as fast. They'd been playing here in town for years, while he had only emerged two weekends ago.

Still, the fantasy was sweet. Renny saw himself playing while Bryce fumed on the bench, waiting to play his paltry few minutes of garbage time when the game was already decided one way or the other. Ha!

It had been fantastic to see the look of pain and fury on Bryce's face at the end of the game today. As his teammates lifted him to their shoulders and chanted his name, Renny had caught a glimpse of Bryce, kicking a Styrofoam cooler to pieces.

Well, good, Renny thought. He deserved it. He'd pretended to be Renny's friend while plotting against him with Turk. "I could have been hurt," Renny muttered.

He had really thought Bryce wanted to be his

friend. "What an idiot I was," Renny said to himself bitterly as he stared at the glow-in-the-dark stars on his ceiling. Why would a popular kid like Bryce Mc-Cormack want to be my friend? No, he was just scoping me out, trying to find my weak points. I guess he thought I didn't have any guts. Well, now he knows I do.

Renny closed his eyes, but sleep just wouldn't come. He thought about what Norm had said about the MVP trophy. It would be nice to get, he conceded.

But then he realized it would also be okay if he didn't win it. It didn't matter to Renny, so long as his team won the championship. He'd had so much success already, it was beyond what had been his wildest dreams at the start of the season. But Bryce . . .

"He's probably been counting on winning the MVP trophy all season," Renny whispered in the dark. All at once, he felt he understood what had made Bryce seek out Turk Walters.

He was desperate, Renny thought. I guess it means more to him than it does to me. And I'll bet when Isaac got hurt, Bryce thought the championship was in the bag. And then I came along. . . .

Suddenly, Renny didn't feel angry with Bryce anymore. Maybe Bryce had suggested to Turk that he foul Renny hard, but a kid like Turk wouldn't have needed much encouragement.

There was one thing Renny didn't understand, though. Bryce had sicced Turk on him, but then he had encouraged Renny to be more aggressive on the field. Was it possible Bryce had had second thoughts about his dirty little trick? If he had, then he couldn't have helped Renny more. Without Bryce's inspiration, Renny would never have raised the level of his game so quickly. He had always been timid on the field; he realized that now. And he would never be timid on the field again — thanks to Bryce.

"Today must have been one of the worst days of his life," Renny breathed. If the Blue Hornets won the championship tomorrow, Renny promised himself that he wouldn't rub it in Bryce's face.

But something told him this play-off wasn't going to be that easy . . . that he hadn't heard the last of Bryce McCormack.

Bryce lay in bed, unable to sleep. His anger was like a red film in front of his eyes. He tossed and turned, burning for revenge.

His whole life he'd been a winner. Now, all of a sudden, he was in danger of being not only a loser, but the goat. If the Yellow Jackets didn't win the championship, everyone would think it was Bryce who had choked under pressure. "He was good," they'd say, "but not good enough."

If the Blue Hornets beat them tomorrow, Renny Harding would win the MVP trophy, no doubt about it. And Coach Harrelson would pick Renny Harding to be JV center striker next fall. Bryce would ride the bench. He would sit there, hoping Renny Harding would go down with a broken ankle, just the way Isaac Mendez had, so that Bryce would get his chance.

Bryce made a face. "I really am a loser," he said out loud. "I nearly got the kid hurt once already — now here I am thinking about him getting injured." He sighed. "I was the best soccer player in this league. So how come he's playing better than me? How come his team won today?"

He realized he'd never asked himself these questions before. It wasn't that Renny had more talent — Bryce was stronger, bigger, more of a natural athlete. But Renny Harding was thinking ahead, and working with his teammates. "Not being a hot dog like me," Bryce mused, recalling Coach Harrelson's description of his play. Renny was the best player on his team, like Bryce, but unlike Bryce, he didn't ignore his teammates and try to do it all himself.

All at once, he wasn't mad at Renny anymore. It had come to Bryce that in order to beat the kid, he had to play like him. Renny expected Bryce to hog the field, not give one of his teammates a chance for glory.

Well, Renny and his Blue Hornets were in for a surprise. Tomorrow, Bryce was going to pull his team back into this thing — by playing soccer Renny Harding's way.

17

The following morning, Renny woke up feeling tired. He hadn't slept much, and his stomach was churning restlessly. He went downstairs, where his mom had made him some pancakes, but the smell of them made him feel even sicker. "I'm not hungry," he told her, pushing his plate away.

"Are you okay?" his mom asked, concerned, coming over to him and feeling his forehead for a fever. "You don't feel hot. But maybe you ought to get back in bed and rest today."

"Are you kidding me?" Renny blurted out. "I have to be at the game!"

"Okay, I know it's very important to you," his mother said soothingly. "But your health is important, too."

"I'm not sick," Renny insisted. "Just tired . . . and a little nervous."

Just then, the phone rang. His mother answered it, and when she heard the voice on the other end of the line, her expression darkened. "Oh, hi," she said unenthusiastically. Then she held out the phone to Renny. "It's your father," she said.

Renny jumped up and took the phone from her. His mom busied herself around the kitchen, making a lot of noise with pots and pans.

"Hi, Dad," Renny said.

"Hey, sport!" his dad's voice came over the line. "How's everything going?"

"Pretty good," Renny said. "My team's in the soccer finals."

"Yeah? That's fantastic! I'll bet you win, too. Are they still letting you start?"

"Yeah, I'm starting every game!" Renny said.

"Good for you. What happened to the other guy ahead of you? Didn't you say you were third string?"

"I was, but he wasn't there one day, so I got to play, and I'm still playing."

"That's my boy!" his dad crowed. "I taught you well, I guess, huh?"

110

"I guess. If you come to our game today, you could see just how well. What do you say?" Renny waited hopefully.

"I wish I could," his dad said sadly. "But I'm leaving for New York tonight. Got a big business meeting there on Monday."

"That's okay, Dad," Renny mumbled. "I understand."

"No, it's not okay, darn it," his dad said. "It stinks. A dad should be there for his son's big game." Renny heard him sigh. "I'm sorry, Renny. I know I've let you down lots of times. . . ."

"No, Dad . . ."

"I have too," his dad insisted. "And none of it was your fault. Look, you go out and play your best. Maybe next time, I'll be able to make it out there to see you."

"Yes, Dad."

"Good luck, son."

"Thanks. Bye." Renny hung up, feeling more down than before.

"What did he want?" his mom asked him.

"Nothing," Renny said. "I've got to go. See you later."

"Are you sure you're feeling well enough?"

"Yeah."

"Renny, you know I've got to work this morning, or I'd love to come and see you play."

"Sure, Mom. It's okay. Bye."

"Bye, honey. Good luck!"

"Thanks." Renny went outside. The morning was gray and foggy, with a little drizzle. Maybe we won't even play, he said to himself. He really did feel sick — weak, and tired, and deeply sad. He hoped they didn't play. Not today.

The game went ahead, even though the drizzle had become steadier. The conditions were slippery, which would be to Renny's advantage. With his moves, the defenders would be slipping and falling all over the place.

"We're gonna be champions!" Jordan Woo was bragging on the sidelines as the players lined up. "Oh, yeah! We're gonna swat the Yellow Jackets! Hornets rule!"

Renny shook his head. Jordan, always so sure they were going to lose, had suddenly become overconfident. "You know, Jordan," he said, "you should try to keep an even keel a little more."

"Huh? What are you talking about?" Jordan asked. "We wiped the floor with them yesterday! We're hot, man! Nobody can stop us!"

Renny gave up. Jordan's moods swung with every breeze.

He could see Bryce warming up across the field. Bryce seemed intensely focused today. He looked totally unaware of his surroundings as he practiced his shots. "This isn't going to be easy," Renny murmured under his breath.

It wasn't. When the starting whistle blew, Bryce took immediate control. He quickly drove the play into the Hornets' end. Renny waited for the ball to come back toward midfield, but it didn't. Bryce got off three shots in a row, and the third found its mark — a big kick that had Chuck Mathes ducking for cover.

Renny led a drive on the next possession, but Sam Plummer, the Yellow Jackets' goalie, made a big save and sent the ball back downfield.

Bryce again led a rush. But this time, to Renny's

amazement, he drew the defense to him, then found the open man on his left wing, Eric Dornquist, with a gorgeous pass. The resulting shot had the Yellow Jackets up 2–0 before five minutes of game time had passed.

Bryce McCormack giving up a chance to shoot on goal? Renny thought. Impossible!

But it wasn't impossible, or the only time in the game Bryce made the unselfish move. He controlled the field that first half — making steals, creating opportunities, and threading passes through double teams to open men. Before the half was over, he had assisted on two more goals.

Down 4–0, Renny finally succeeded in rallying the Hornets for a goal, finding John Singleman with a well-placed corner kick to make the score 4–1 at halftime. But as they gathered around Coach McMaster, Renny could see defeat written on the faces of all his teammates. They had already accepted in their hearts that today was not their day.

Today was Bryce McCormack's day, and there seemed to be nothing Renny could do about it.

18

Man, you were amazing! That's the best I've ever seen you play!" Eric Dornquist said to Bryce as they downed sports drinks at halftime.

Bryce felt as if he were dreaming. All through the first half, he'd seen the whole field at once, as though he were hovering over it. Somehow, he knew where to go, which way to dribble, when to fake, and when to bull ahead. He'd been patient with his shots and unselfish in his passing. "Yeah, I guess I played pretty good."

"The game's not over!" Coach Hickey barked at him. But Bryce could see he was smiling. "Keep your heads in it, and we'll win it!" He patted Bryce's shoulder. "That's my boy," he said fondly.

Bryce grinned.

When play resumed, he focused his energy out

onto the field, muscling the opposing players aside to get control of the ball. Once he had it, he passed it off to the midfielders and tried to get open for the pass. Soon he was back in the groove.

On the next play, he made a quick pass to Eric, then scooted ahead to receive the return pass. He got there just in time, and right near the goal. The shot was easy, too. Right past the goalie before he could even leave his feet.

Bryce let out a whoop as he ran back into position to await the start of play. Why had he been so worried all this time? Renny Harding was an okay player, but put Bryce's best game against Renny's and it was no contest!

The final score was 6–2. Bryce had scored three goals and assisted on the other three. This time it was he, not Renny Harding, who was carried off the field on the shoulders of his teammates. Renny had finished the day with one measly goal and one assist.

They were even now. Each boy had had one great game and one lousy one. Each team had beaten the other convincingly. The series was knotted at a game apiece, with everything riding on tomorrow's contest.

"It's gonna be another blowout," Bryce told his teammates quietly as they gathered around the coach.

"Let's not let them get back into it now," Coach Hickey told his team. "We've got the momentum; let's not give it up. Play the same game tomorrow as you did today, and we'll be the champions."

The team gave a huge cheer that was echoed back to them by their fans. Bryce looked up into the stands, where all the parents were sitting. A lot of them were clapping encouragement, calling out their kids' names. Some of them were even waving to him, calling out his name, even though he wasn't their kid.

That was nice, Bryce thought. They all cared about him because he was a good athlete. But they didn't really know him. Would they still like him if they did?

Suddenly, Bryce found himself thinking about his dad. That long, dark, scraggly hair hanging straight down behind his ears. The smile with the deep-set eyes and the crooked teeth. He'd been such a cool dad when Bryce was little. Now he hadn't had a phone call from him in almost two months and hadn't seen him in more than a year. Why had he gone?

Bryce blinked back the tears, angry at himself for letting the memories overcome him. He should be celebrating, but instead he was down in the dumps. What did it all matter, if your parents weren't there to see how well you'd done?

"Hey, kid!" Bryce turned around at the sound of the voice behind him. He knew that voice. It was Coach Harrelson!

"That was some mighty fine soccer you played out there today," he told Bryce.

Bryce tried to say thanks, but nothing came out, so he just nodded.

"You seem pretty glum. Anything the matter?" the coach asked, his brow furrowing.

Bryce shook his head and smiled.

"Good," Coach Harrelson said. "You should be proud of yourself today. Not many boys have your kind of talent, and if you can keep using your head the way you just did, I see great things in your future. Great things." He stuck out his hand.

Bryce reached out and shook it. "Th-thanks, sir!" he managed to say.

"I'll be back to see you tomorrow. Good luck out there." The coach winked, then turned and walked away.

Bryce was floating on air. He looked across the field and caught sight of Renny walking away, looking down at the ground as he went. He was alone. Apparently his parents hadn't come to see him play, either.

To his surprise, Bryce found himself feeling sorry for Renny — and angry at himself for messing up what could have been a great friendship. Right then and there, he vowed that if he ever got the chance, he'd make Renny see that he was sorry for having betrayed him.

19

Renny had just gotten off the phone with Jordan Woo. For half an hour, he'd been trying to convince Jordan that the Hornets still had a chance to win the championship. "Not unless Bryce comes down with appendicitis or something!" Jordan had moaned. "Did you see him today? Forget it!"

"We've beaten them two out of three," Renny pointed out. "I just had a bad game, that's all."

"You? *You* had a bad game? I don't call getting two goals a bad game. Ha! I wish I could score a goal just once!"

"It was only one goal," Renny corrected him. "I dished off to John on the other one."

"Big deal," Jordan said. "It was the rest of us who

stunk up the joint. Did you see how our midfield and defense collapsed when Bryce came at them?"

"Not really," Renny said. "I was busy trying to get free downfield."

And on and on it went until, finally, he told Jordan he had to get off the phone. The call had made his head swim, so he decided to go for a walk.

Out of habit, he headed for the soccer field. He was rounding the corner of the clubhouse when he ran smack into Bryce. The two boys stared at each other.

"Hey," Bryce said finally. "What's up?"

Renny shrugged. "Just decided to take a walk, that's all."

"Me, too." Bryce squinted at the setting sun. "Listen, wanna go get a bite to eat? Maybe Conroy's?"

Renny was surprised but tried to hide it. "Yeah, all right," he replied as nonchalantly as he could.

Soon they were walking down the street side by side, silently. Renny waited for Bryce to say something.

Finally, he did. "I saw you after the game today. You looked kind of down."

Renny shrugged. "We lost," he said.

"I know, but . . . well, I noticed you were alone. Your mom didn't come down to see you?"

"She works on Saturdays. She's a real estate agent. It's a big day for showing houses."

"Same with my mom," Bryce said, smiling sadly.

"She's in real estate, too?" Renny asked.

"Nah, she works in a store," Bryce explained. "Busy, busy. Never has time to come see a game."

"I don't think my mom's into soccer, really," Renny said. "She pretends to get excited about it, but I can tell her heart isn't in it. My dad used to take me to all my games. . . ."

"Uh-huh," Bryce said. "When's the last time he saw you play?"

"Last year in Haverford," Renny said. "What about yours?"

"Third grade," Bryce said.

"Wow!" Renny couldn't disguise his surprise. "How come he never comes to see you?"

"He lives way over in Oakmont. That's a good three hours from here. No time for Bryce Junior."

"Still," Renny said, "he could come and see you play once in a while."

Bryce frowned. "Let's change the subject, okay?"

"Okay." Renny was silent for a moment. "You were awesome today," he said finally.

Bryce looked at him sideways, then shrugged. "Thanks. I was mad. At you."

"Me?"

"For beating us Friday afternoon."

"Oh. Well, sorry," Renny said.

"Get out of here; you're not sorry — you shouldn't be, anyway," Bryce said.

The two boys fell silent again.

"Listen," Bryce said suddenly, coming to a stop on the pavement. "About what happened with Turk Walters — I just want to say I'm sorry I was such a jerk."

"Uh-huh," Renny said, not letting Bryce off the hook just yet.

"I guess I was afraid of you getting into the play-offs and playing better than me," Bryce went on. "Which still could happen, I guess."

"You want to know something funny?" Renny said. "I think the reason I played so good on Friday afternoon was because Turk told me the whole story right before the game."

"I was afraid of that," Bryce said. "I never told him to try and hurt you, by the way."

"You said that already."

"Yeah. Well. I guess I still feel bad about it."

"Forget it," Renny said. "I came out of it okay, right? No harm done. You won't do it again."

"I sure hope not," Bryce agreed. "Funny, though, how we both play better when we're angry. I mean, now that we've talked, who are we going to be angry with?"

"I think we should both just go out there and play confident. If we both do our best, it'll come down to how well the guys behind us play."

"Yeah, I like that," Bryce said. Then he stopped walking again. "Listen, I don't really feel like ice cream. You?"

"Nah," Renny agreed. "Maybe tomorrow, after the game."

"Yeah!" Bryce said. "No matter who wins, okay?"

"Sure thing," Renny said, putting out his hand. Bryce took it. "So we're friends, no matter what, right?"

"You got it," Bryce said, shaking Renny's hand

hard. "You know something else? You're better than Isaac Mendez ever was."

"Really?"

"Really. I mean it. He never made me take my game to a higher level the way you did."

"Huh. I guess that goes both ways. You helped me raise my game, too."

"Cool." Bryce smiled. "Well, I guess I'll head home from here, okay?"

"Sure. See you tomorrow."

"Right." Bryce turned to go, then stopped and turned back. "Good luck," he said. "I mean you personally, not the Hornets, of course."

"Of course. Good luck to you, too. See you on the field."

Renny stood there for a while, watching Bryce's figure retreat into the gathering darkness of the spring evening. Then he turned for home.

When he got there, he picked up the phone and dialed long-distance information. "The number of a McCormack in Oakmont, please," he said.

"Do you have a first name for the party?" the operator asked.

"Can you give me all of them?"

"I have twenty-seven McCormacks in Oakmont, sir, and fifteen MacCormacks. Would you like all of them?"

"Uh . . . no, I guess not," Renny said, defeated. Then he remembered something Bryce had said: *"No time for Bryce Junior."*

"Could you try under the first name of Bryce?" Renny asked the operator.

"I have only one B. McCormack. Would you like that one?"

Renny took the number and dialed it. It rang four times. Then a machine picked up. "Hello, this is Bryce," a man's voice said. "Leave a message, including your number, and I'll get back to you." A beep followed.

"Hello," Renny said. "Mr. McCormack, I'm a friend of your son's, and I just wanted you to know he's got a big soccer game tomorrow morning — the biggest one of his life. He's a great player, Mr. McCormack, the best. And . . . and you really should see him play, at least once."

He took a breath. Tears were in his eyes, and Renny couldn't figure out why. And then he knew —

it was as if he were talking to his own dad, except he was saying words he would never say to his dad.

"You should go to the game," Renny said, trying to keep his voice steady. "Or at least call to wish him good luck." Renny paused a moment. "I hope you get this message . . . and I hope you listen. You have a really good kid for a son. You should treat him better."

Renny slowly hung up and wiped his eyes with the back of his hand. Then he went into the kitchen to give his mom a hug.

20

The stands were packed on both sides of the field, and all along the sidelines people were camped out to watch the big game. There was a sound system with a microphone, and the league commissioner was there to announce the game and give out the trophies afterward.

Bryce recognized kids from every team in the league. A lot of them came up to wish him good luck, but some didn't. Bryce knew why. At one time or another, he'd probably shown them up — outplayed them, dissed them, fouled them, or just plain made them look bad.

It would take a long time to get people to notice he'd changed, Bryce realized. But something inside him *had* changed. Renny Harding had shown him that you could be a great competitor without playing as if you were the only one on the field.

Well, today he was going to show what he was made of. Bryce didn't feel nervous, really — more like he was flying above it all, like in the last game. He knew he was going to have a good one.

Renny huddled with his teammates and their coach. They all looked at each other, including Isaac Mendez, who was there in uniform, with his ankle in a soft cast now. "You ready to go get that championship trophy?" the coach asked his team.

The Blue Hornets put their hands together and raised their voices in a mighty shout. "Goooo, Blue!!"

Even Jordan Woo seemed excited. "Still betting on the Yellow Jackets?" Renny asked him with a wry smile.

"Kind of," Jordan admitted. "But I figure we might as well go down fighting."

"Jordan!" Renny said, grabbing both Jordan's shoulders and shaking him. "Snap out of it! Today's our day; I can feel it!"

"*Your* day, maybe," Jordan said. "Our day, mmm . . . I don't know."

"The odds are fifty-fifty actually," Norm Harvey said, stepping forward. He was wearing a Blue Hornets uniform, too — with the number 00 on it.

Renny had to laugh. "Hey, cool uniform, dude!" he said. "You've got to admit, there are no uniforms in chess."

"Please," Norm said, rolling his eyes. "I am only wearing this ridiculous thing in support of the team."

"Jordan," Renny said. "Speak to Norm here about team spirit, okay? I've got to get out there."

He ran out onto the field with the other starters and took his position. The ref blew his whistle, and the big game began.

On his first rush, Bryce left three Hornets on the ground where they fell, skidding, while trying to stay with him. He faked the shot, then passed to Eric Dornquist, who one-timed it past the goalie for the first score of the game.

Bryce clapped his hands once, then trotted back toward midfield. He felt no desire to do his usual "victory dance" this time. He let Eric hotdog it around the field. The team was only up one goal. Bryce wasn't ready to celebrate yet. This game was far from over.

Sure enough, Renny broke free off a throw-in and forced a corner kick. Bryce could only watch helplessly as the ball stayed in the Yellow Jackets' end, fought over by a swarm of players from both teams. He knew the Hornets had scored when the roar went up from that end of the field. And he knew who had gotten the goal when they started shouting his name: "Ren-ny! Ren-ny! Ren-ny!"

Bryce was the next one to draw blood, though. His team kept control after the whistle, and he drifted downfield to the right of the ball, which was being dribbled by Eric Dornquist on left wing.

Bryce saw an opening behind the defender, called out to Eric, and ran into the gap. The pass from Eric found him perfectly in midstride. Bryce kicked the ball softly toward the front of the goal, then beat the goalie to it as he came out to smother the ball. The shot dribbled into the net. Bryce felt himself rise into the air as he tripped over the goalie, did a full somersault, and came up standing. He raised his arms in triumph as the crowd applauded. Now it was his name they were chanting!

Renny was really into it now. He promised himself that this next goal was his and his alone. The Hornets couldn't afford to allow the Yellow Jackets a two-goal lead, and with Bryce taking a breather, now was the best time to tie up the game again.

Renny deliberately went out of position to his right, causing a small crowd to congregate around him and away from the ball. Then he seized his moment and rushed back to center, three steps ahead of the defenders. "Over here!" he shouted to the left-winger, John Singleman.

John sent the ball downfield, and Renny ran to keep up with it. It landed in front of him, bouncing toward the last defender. Renny got there first, headed the ball over the defender, and deked around his left. The defender whirled around, too late. Renny already had control of the ball, with only the goalie to beat.

Renny took his time. He could feel the other defenders racing toward him. At the last moment, he faked twice, then kicked. Just as he'd guessed, the goalie had gone for the second fake, thinking it would be his real move. Renny had outmaneuvered him, and the game was tied, 2–2!

It stayed that way until halftime. Renny collapsed on the sidelines, exhausted. He had played the entire half and had never stopped running.

"I'm holding you out for the start of the second half," Coach McMaster told him. "You're all flushed. Drink some fluids. Don't worry; I'll get you back in there."

Renny didn't argue. He knew the coach was right. Bryce McCormack was big and strong enough to play the whole game without any more rest, but Renny wasn't. He only hoped the game stayed close till he got back in.

"Dad?"

Bryce couldn't believe it. He was staring into the eyes of his father, who was looking back at him through tears.

"Hello, son," he said softly. "I've been sitting here the whole time, just watching you." He smiled. "You keep it up and you're going to have you a trophy. You know something? You're even better than I was when I was your age."

Bryce's eyes widened. "Really? You mean that?" Bryce had seen the old photographs, the dusty trophies. His dad had been all-state in high school, in three different sports!

"I'm sorry I haven't been around to see you more often, son," his dad said. "I don't know . . . sometimes I think what's going on in my life is so important." He laughed without joy. "Funny, huh? I guess this is what's really important, right?"

Bryce nodded and swallowed hard. "I'm glad you came, Dad," he said, and the two of them hugged. His father ran a hand through Bryce's hair and said, "I'm going to make it my business to get to know you again. . . . If that's okay with you."

"It's great, Dad," Bryce whispered, hugging him tighter.

"Yellow Jackets!" Coach Hickey shouted. "Let's go! Gather round!"

"I've got to go," Bryce said.

"You get out there and nail it down, Junior," his father said. "I'll be rooting for you."

With Renny on the sidelines, the game rapidly began to tilt in favor of the Yellow Jackets. When Bryce

134

hit an incredible shot, with two defenders on him, to put his team back into the lead, Renny sprang up and ran over to Coach McMaster. "Put me back in, Coach!" he demanded. "I've got to get back in there!"

"All right," McMaster said. "Singleman! Come out for a breather!"

"What? Why, Coach? We need him on the wing!"

"I've got to get my subs in there sometime," Coach McMaster explained. "League rules — everyone gets at least ten minutes of playing time, finals or no finals."

Shaking his head but understanding, Renny headed out onto the field. Possession kept changing hands over the next five minutes, until finally John Singleman was put back into the game. Now that Renny had some real help up front, the Hornets were able to sustain a rush. It ended with Singleman putting a corner kick right onto Renny's foot, ten feet in front of the goalie. One swift kick later, the score was tied again!

"We're gonna win! We're gonna win! Oh, yes!" Renny could hear Jordan Woo screaming. He paid no attention. With time running down, he knew he had to keep his focus on the game.

Bryce McCormack was causing all kinds of trouble in the Hornets' zone now. Renny, not wanting to give the Yellow Jackets the lead again, ran back to help out on defense. He could hear his coach yelling at him to stay up front, but he knew he had to get back there and give his overwhelmed defensemen some support.

He had the advantage of surprise, and when he came up behind Bryce, it was easy to knock the ball away from him. "Hey!" Bryce yelled. "What are you doing back here?"

Renny didn't answer. He was already in hot pursuit of the ball. He got to it just before it went out of bounds, then spun around and kicked it downfield to John Singleman.

By the time he got into the Yellow Jackets' zone, the ball had already been shot and the rebound was coming right toward him. Renny headed it back toward the goal and rushed in to keep up the pressure. It was too much for Sam Plummer, the harried Yellow Jackets goalie, who shouted for help — too late. Renny busted a shot over Sam's left shoulder that caught the net just underneath the top bar. The Hornets had their first lead of the game!

"Two minutes left!" the referee alerted the teams.

"Everyone up front!" the Yellow Jackets' coach yelled. "This is it! Get it to Bryce!"

Renny heard him and called out to the other forwards to get back and help. With all the Yellow Jacket defensemen downfield, the Hornets' defense would be outmanned and outgunned. It was a desperate ploy, and it was dangerous. It meant the play would be in the Hornets' end — and that, of course, meant some risk. Still, if the Hornets could fall back and jam up the passing lanes, Bryce would have little chance of getting off a good shot in time.

Renny made it his business to guard Bryce one-on-one. Bryce saw him coming this time and smiled confidently. He certainly didn't look to Renny like a beaten man.

So. This was it, Bryce thought, as he saw Renny coming at him. It was now or never, with less than two minutes left to play. There was only one thought on Bryce's mind — score, and make it fast. He put a move on Renny that was so sudden Renny slid to the ground and tumbled head over heels. "Yeah!" Bryce shouted as he deked two more Hornet defenders.

He was zigging and zagging toward the goal but

subtly allowing the defense to push him to the left, clearing the middle for his Yellow Jacket teammates.

Then, when the defenders had fully committed to him, Bryce seized the moment. He went into his patented spin move, the one he'd shown Renny, and lifted the ball into the air, where he headed it over the defense and into the wide-open middle.

"Get back in position!" Coach McMaster was screaming. But it was too late. The Yellow Jackets had a three-on-one rush going, and Bryce, along with the stunned defenders, ran toward the play.

There was a hard shot, which the goalie got a hand on. Then there was one rebound, then another. Renny Harding put his body in front of a fourth shot, but the rebound came straight to Bryce.

This was the moment he'd been waiting for. He reared back his right leg and smashed a blur of a shot right into the corner of the net, just as the ref blew his whistle signaling the end of regulation time!

"Tie game!" the ref shouted. "Fifteen-minute overtime."

*   *   *

Ten minutes went by, and the teams traded one more goal each, with Renny setting up John Singleman, and Bryce feeding Eric Dornquist. Time was winding down.

Renny knew what would happen now. If nobody came up with a goal in the next five minutes or so, there would be a shoot-out. Each team would get five shots at the goal, and whoever got the most goals would win the game — and the championship. Each team would choose five shooters, for one shot apiece.

Sure enough, the rest of the overtime period was scoreless, and the five minutes went by in no time.

"Shoot-out!" the ref shouted. "Teams, select your shooters!"

Coach McMaster picked his five shooters. "Wilkes first, then Singleman, then Bowie, then Charlie, and then Renny."

Renny was worried. What if the Hornets were out of the running before he even got his chance to shoot? But he realized he had no control over that.

Renny trotted out onto the field. There was Bryce, facing him across the center line. "I'm going last. You?" Bryce asked.

"Also," Renny confirmed.

The two boys shook hands, and the ref flipped a coin. "Call it, Hornets," he said.

"Heads," Renny called.

"Heads it is." The ref turned to Renny. "Do you want to shoot first or second?"

"Second," Renny said.

The first Yellow Jacket to shoot was Eric Dornquist. He placed the ball at the top of the Hornets' zone. Chuck Mathes braced himself in goal. Eric shot, and the ball flew toward the net. Chuck leaped into the air, his arms stretched skyward, and deflected the shot.

"Way to go, Chuck!" Renny screamed.

But the first Hornets' shooter did no better, his shot skimming off the side of his foot and dribbling harmlessly into the goalie's arms.

The second Yellow Jacket to shoot was Steve Weintraub. He took a big shot. Chuck deflected it, but it found the top of the net and went in. A groan went up from the Hornets' sideline, a cheer from across the field, where the Yellow Jackets began jumping up and down.

"Go get 'em, John," Renny said. Singleman gave

him a high five, then trotted out onto the field. John had a wicked shot, and he showed it now, putting a zinger into the corner of the net. The score was 1–1, with three shots each left to go.

None of the next three shooters managed to put the ball in the net. The score was still 1–1 when Charlie Ebbetts took his turn. As the Yellow Jackets' goalie steeled himself, Charlie wound up as if to give the ball a mighty kick.

Sam, fooled by the motion, went for the phantom kick. But Charlie hadn't sent the ball into the air after all. Instead, he blasted it on the ground — and right into the net! It was 2–1, Hornets, with just Bryce and Renny left to go!

Bryce went first. Renny's heart was pounding in his chest as he watched his friend size up the goalie. Chuck bounced from foot to foot impatiently.

Bryce did what he did best — he used his power and strength to bull the ball right past Chuck. The score was now tied.

"Come on, Renny!" Coach McMaster shouted above the roar of the crowd. "Put it in, and we're champs!"

Renny took the ball. This was it — if he failed, the

score would still be tied and the teams would select other shooters. The outcome would be out of his hands, and he would have to watch from the sidelines while the game, and the season, was decided.

This was his chance, and Renny knew it. He stood poised, waiting for the whistle. When it came, he moved with lightning speed and kicked as hard as he could. Sam leaped into the air, extending his arms to try and deflect the ball, but it hit the post — then caromed across the goal, finding the net just over the goal line. The game was over! The Hornets had won it all!

Bryce sank to the ground in disbelief. The season was over, and his team had lost!

In the past, Bryce knew, he would have thrown a tantrum right about now, breaking things wherever he could find them. But Bryce didn't feel like breaking anything now. He just felt stunned, and drained, and tired.

His father was standing over him, gazing at him fondly. "I'm real proud of you, Junior," he said, crouching and putting his head next to Bryce's. A fatherly arm came around Bryce's shoulder. "It doesn't matter so much who won. You played your heart out. It was a beautiful thing to see."

They hugged, and Bryce felt the tears coming. They came and came. He hadn't cried like this since . . . since third grade.

Finally, he wiped the tears away and stood up. "I've got to go shake hands," he told his dad. "Wait for me, okay?"

"Sure thing," his dad said, releasing him with a smile.

Bryce went over and lined up with his team. "Good game," they told each of the elated Hornets in turn.

"Good game," Bryce told Renny, stopping to grab his hand. "Really good game."

"You, too," Renny said with a smile. "Ice-cream sundaes later, remember?"

"Uh-huh," Bryce said, managing to smile back.

Coach Hickey gathered the Yellow Jackets around him. "You boys have been the best team I've ever coached," he said. "I'm sorry we didn't win, but I'm not sorry we played the way we did today. We lost to a great effort by a very good team. That's soccer for you. But you can all hold your heads up. And I've got a trophy for each one of you when we have the team picnic next week."

The team managed a cheer, then gave each other high fives for the season they'd had — a first-place finish and a great play-off.

A man with a big camera came up to Bryce. "Hey, Number Ten, I want you for a photograph for the *Crestmont Herald.* Come on over here."

He led Bryce over to where Renny was standing. "The two of you, pose together with the ball between you. That's it," the photographer said. "Now, kind of growl at each other. That's it. . . ."

He snapped the picture, and both boys cracked up.

Then the commissioner of the soccer league got on the sound system. "It's time to present the championship and MVP trophies," he announced.

First, the big team trophy was given to Coach Mc-Master, who handed it to Bill Kelly of Kelly's Plumbing, the team's sponsor. "This'll be featured in our big display window!" Mr. Kelly crowed, holding the trophy over his head to cheers from the crowd.

"And now, it's time for the Most Valuable Player

award," the commissioner announced. "This year, we had a tough decision to make. . . ."

Bryce stood there frozen, hanging on the commissioner's every word.

"But there was only one trophy to give out, so we couldn't split the award. Therefore, the trophy goes to . . . Renny Harding of the league champions, Kelly's Plumbing Blue Hornets!"

It took Bryce a second to recover; then he began clapping and cheering, leading the applause for Renny, who looked as if he was going to faint while receiving the trophy. The kid is really stunned, Bryce realized. He can't believe he got it.

Bryce had figured Renny would get the award. After all, he was the best player on the winning team, and that was how MVPs got chosen. Bryce didn't feel hurt by it. The pain of losing the game had been much worse.

Renny was coming toward him with the trophy. "Bryce," he said. "You should really have won this. I don't know why —"

"Cut it out," Bryce said. "You deserve it. You guys won. That's life."

"Hey, you two!"

Bryce and Renny turned. Coach Harrelson nodded at them. "Yeah, you two guys. Let me congratulate both of you."

He shook each of their hands, then turned to Renny. "Listen, young fella, I hope I'll be seeing you at the tryouts for the JV team next season. I suspect you'd do quite well as my center striker."

"Are you kidding me?" Renny gasped. "I mean, thank you."

Now Bryce was *really* hurt. The coach's words had been like daggers going through his gut. He'd practically promised Renny that he'd start at center striker!

There went Bryce's last hope. He'd lost out to Renny where it really counted.

"And as for you, young man." The coach turned to Bryce.

Bryce looked at him, blinking. What was he going to do — offer Bryce a nice warm seat on the JV bench?

"You've got an extraordinary package of skills," Coach Harrelson told Bryce. "I'll bet Coach Johnson will find a starting spot for you on the front line of the varsity team."

"What?!" Bryce couldn't believe what he'd just heard — the varsity! As a *freshman!*

"It wouldn't be at center striker, you understand. My guess is he's gonna go with Curtis Jenkins. You'd have to take right wing, with Nick Vaccarella on the left."

Bryce stuttered his thanks, and the two boys watched Coach Harrelson leave to congratulate the coaches.

"I'm about ready for a sundae, how 'bout you?" Bryce asked Renny.

"Definitely!" Renny said, nodding happily. "We've got a lot to celebrate."

"And my dad is buying," Bryce told him.

Renny stared at him, wide-eyed. "He's here?" he asked.

Bryce nodded as his dad came up behind him. "Dad, I want you to meet my new friend, Renny Harding."

"Pleasure," Bryce's dad told Renny. "Funny, I feel like I know you already. . . ."

Out of the corner of his eye, Bryce thought he saw his dad wink at Renny. But why would he do that? he wondered.

147

Nah. Maybe he'd only imagined it. Anyway, what did it matter? Bryce felt like the whole world was his friend today. And as for Renny — the two of them would be cheering each other on all next season. And someday, when Renny got to the varsity squad, they'd even get to be teammates.

The three of them, Bryce, his dad, and Renny, walked toward Conroy's. As they went, Renny and Bryce talked excitedly about the great plays they'd made that day, and about the future.

Bryce felt his dad's arm around his shoulder and smiled. He'd lost the championship, and the MVP award, too. But life was still good — it was very, very good.

Matt Christopher

Kobe Bryant

Terrell Davis

Julie Foudy

Jeff Gordon

Wayne Gretzky

Ken Griffey Jr.

Mia Hamm

Tony Hawk

Grant Hill

Derek Jeter

Randy Johnson

Michael Jordan

Tara Lipinski

Mark McGwire

Greg Maddux

Hakeem Olajuwon

Alex Rodriguez

Briana Scurry

Sammy Sosa

Venus and
Serena Williams

Tiger Woods

Steve Young

The #1 Sports Series for Kids

Read them all!

All available in paperback from Little, Brown and Company